7 day   1 7

j398   Manning-Sanders, Ruth.
M   A book of witches. New York,
          Dutton, c1965.
                                    4.50

J

          I.Title.

A Book of Witches

A BOOK OF
Witches

Ruth Manning-Sanders

DRAWINGS BY

Robin Jacques

E. P. Dutton & Co., Inc.   New York

First published in the U.S.A., 1966 by E.P. Dutton & Co., Inc.
Copyright, ©, 1965 by Ruth Manning-Sanders
All rights reserved. Printed in the U.S.A.

Seventh Printing, July 1972

Library of Congress Catalog Card Number: 66-14685

Foreword

There are good witches and bad witches; but the number of the bad witches is great, and the number of the good witches is small. And since the business of the good witches is mainly to undo the mischief made by the bad ones, their stories are not very interesting. In all the stories in this book, you will only find one mention of a good witch, and that is at the beginning of the Norwegian tale of *Tatterhood*. And you will see that had the queen done exactly what this good little witch bade her, there would be no more story to tell. But the bad witches cause exciting things to happen.

These bad witches are, of course, exceedingly powerful: they can fly through the air on broomsticks, or on stalks of ragwort, or even on old jars; they can raise tempests; they can cross the sea in stone boats, or kneading troughs, or sieves; in their great cauldrons they can brew magic potions that put spells on their enemies; and they can turn themselves, and other people, into pigs, or geese, or cats, or hares, or into any other shape they fancy.

In some fairy tales, too, there are wicked witch-maidens, who are surpassingly beautiful; and these maidens are perhaps the most dangerous witches of all. Anyone, meeting with a humpy-backed old woman, with a great hooked nose, little red eyes, huge leering mouth, and craggy chin, might recognize such a creature for the witch she was, and so be on his guard. But if confronted with a sweet-voiced maiden of dazzling beauty – who would suspect evil? You have to be a very sharp fellow, like the hero of the Bohemian story, *Johnny and the Witch-Maidens*, to recognize the real nature of these fascinating and seemingly innocent damsels. And even Johnny might have been deceived by their charms, had he not been forewarned by his poor old master.

Some witches have big families of daughters, and these daughters are usually very stupid – you will find thirteen of these silly daughters in the Danish story of *Esben and the Witch*. But it is rarely that you come across a witch who has a son. You might think that to be the son of a witch was not a happy fate; but, provided that the son is good, he has at least one advantage: he picks up a lot of magic from his witch-mother, and so is able to foil her evil spells. One such son is the attractive Benvenuto, in the Italian story of *Prunella*.

Of the rest of the stories, *Rapunzel*, *Lazy Hans*, *The Donkey Lettuce* and *Hansel and Gretel*, all come from Germany. *The White Dove* is a Danish story, and *The Old Witch* an English one; *The Twins and the Snarling Witch* comes from Russia, and *The Blackstairs Mountain* from Ireland.

Now in all these stories, as in the fairy tales about witches in general, you may be sure of one thing: however terrible the witches may seem – and whatever power they may have to lay spells on people and to work mischief – they are always defeated. So that though, at some point in the story, you may find the hero or heroine in utter distress, you need never fear for them. Because it is the absolute and very comforting rule of the fairy tale that the good and brave shall be rewarded, and that bad people shall come to a bad end.

Contents

1 · The Old Witch

There were two sisters who lived at home with their father and mother. And it so happened that the father fell sick and was not able to work. So there they were, without much money, and getting poorer every day. One sister moaned and wept and grumbled, but the other sister said, 'Well, if father can't work, I can. I will go into service, and all the money I earn I will send home.'

So she packed up some clothes in a bundle, kissed her father and mother, said good-bye to her grumpy sister, and set off for the town.

She called at this house and that house, but no one wanted a servant, so she walked on into the country. And she came to a place where there was an oven. The oven was hot, and it was full of loaves.

And the loaves called out of the oven, 'Little girl, little girl, take us out, take us out! We have been baking for seven years, and no one has come to take us out.'

So the girl took out the loaves, laid them on the ground, and went on her way.

She hadn't gone far when she came to a cow standing by itself in a field, with a lot of milk pails round it. And the cow said, 'Little girl, little girl, milk me, milk me! Seven years I have been waiting here, and no one has come to milk me.'

So the girl milked the cow into the pails. Being thirsty, she drank some of the milk, and the rest she left in the pails.

She went on a little farther and she came to an apple tree. The branches of the apple tree were so loaded with fruit that they were bowed to the ground. And the apple tree said, 'Little girl, little girl, shake me, shake me! Seven years have I waited for someone to shake down my fruit, and my branches are so heavy that they will surely break!'

'You poor tree, of course I will shake you,' said the girl. And she shook all the apples off the tree, propped up its branches, and left the apples in a heap on the ground.

She went a little farther and came to a house. She tapped at the door and a witch opened it. The girl asked if she wanted a servant, and the witch said she did, and that if the girl pleased her, and did what she was told, she would pay her good wages.

So the girl took service with the witch. The witch said, 'Sweep and dust, cook and wash, and be careful to keep the hearth-stones clean, for as you see they are made of marble and very precious. But one thing you must never do. You must never look up the chimney, or you will repent it.'

The girl worked hard, and she worked well. The witch was pleased with her; but she didn't pay the girl any wages. 'If I do,' thought she, 'the girl will take them and go home, and I shall lose her.'

Well, all went on smoothly and dully for a time. And then, one day when the witch was out, and the girl was on her knees cleaning the hearth, she forgot what the witch had said, and she looked up the chimney.

Mercy me! *Chink, chink, clitter, clatter* – a great bag full of money came tumbling down.

The girl looked up the chimney again. She looked up many times, and every time – down fell a bag of money.

'Oh!' thought the girl, 'this money will keep them in comfort at home for years and years!' And she gathered up as many bags as she could carry and ran out to go home.

When she had gone some way, she heard the witch coming after her and shrieking at her to stop. So she ran to the apple tree, and said:

> '*Apple tree, apple tree, hide me,*
> *So the old witch can't find me;*
> *If she does, she'll pick my bones,*
> *And bury me under the marble stones.*'

And the apple tree said, 'Climb up among my branches, and I will bend them over you.'

The girl climbed up, and the apple tree criss-crossed its branches over her so that she was completely hidden.

By and by up came the witch and said:

'Tree of mine, tree of mine,
Have you seen a girl
With a willy-willy wag, and a long-tailed bag,
Who's stolen my money, all I had?'

And the apple tree answered, 'No, mother; not for seven years.'

So the witch went off another way. And the girl climbed down from the apple tree and ran on. Just as she got to the place where the cow was grazing, she heard the witch coming after her again. So she ran to the cow, and said:

'Cow, cow, hide me,
So the old witch can't find me;
If she does, she'll pick my bones,
And bury me under the marble stones.'

And the cow said, 'Get behind the milk pails.'

The girl crouched down behind the milk pails; and the cow gave the pails a kick, and tumbled them on top of her. Up came the witch, and said:

'Cow of mine, cow of mine,
Have you seen a girl,
With a willy-willy wag, and a long-tailed bag,
Who's stolen my money, all I had?'

And the cow answered, 'No, mother; not for seven years.'

So the witch turned off on another path, and the girl came out from under the milk pails, and ran on. She had got as far as the place where the oven was, when she heard the witch coming after her again. So she said:

'Oven, oven, hide me,
So the old witch can't find me;
If she does, she'll break my bones,
And bury me under the marble stones.'

The girl thought to creep into the oven, but the oven said, 'No, no! There's the baker, go and ask him.'

So the girl ran to the baker, and he hid her under a pile of firewood.

When the witch came up, she was looking, here, there, and everywhere. She saw the baker standing by the oven, and said:

> '*Man of mine, man of mine,*
> *Have you seen a girl,*
> *With a willy-willy wag, and a long-tailed bag,*
> *Who's stolen my money, all I had?*'

And the baker said, 'Look in the oven.'

The witch went to look in the oven, and the oven said, 'Get in, and look in the farthest corner.' So the witch got in, and the oven slammed its door, and kept the witch inside for so long that the girl was able to get safely home.

My word – weren't there rejoicings in her home over those bags of money the girl had brought with her! The family were able now to live in comfort. The father got well again, the girl and her sister had pretty clothes to wear, and all went merrily. But the girl's sister wasn't content. She wanted more money and more money. She thought she would go into service with the witch, and get some money bags for herself.

So off she went. And when she came to the oven there it was, full of loaves again. And the loaves called to her, 'Little girl, little girl, take us out, take us out! Seven years we have been baking, and no one has come to take us out.'

But the girl answered, 'No, I don't want to burn my fingers,' and she walked on. She came to the cow, and the cow called to her, 'Little girl, little girl, do milk me! Seven years I have been waiting, and no one has come to milk me.'

But the girl answered, 'No, I can't stop to milk you. I'm in a hurry.'

She went on, and came to the apple tree. The branches of the apple tree were so loaded with fruit that they were bowed to the ground. And the apple tree called out, 'Little girl, little girl, shake me, do! Seven years I have been waiting, and now my branches are so heavy that they will surely break.'

The girl answered, 'No, I can't stop. Another day, perhaps.' And she hurried on and came to the witch's house.

The witch took her into service, and said to her, as she had said to her sister, 'Sweep and dust, cook and wash, and be careful to keep the hearth-stones clean, for as you see they are made of marble and very precious. But one thing you must never do. You must never look up the chimney, or you will repent it.'

The girl laughed to herself, and thought, 'We'll see who repents it – you or I!'

And the very first time the witch went out the girl looked up the chimney.

Chink, chink, clitter, clatter – down fell a bag of money. The girl looked up the chimney many times; and each time – *chink, chink,* down plumped a bag of money. The girl gathered up as many bags as she could carry, and then ran out to go home. She had got as far as the apple tree, when she heard the witch coming screeching after her, so she said:

> *'Apple tree, apple tree, hide me,*
> *So the old witch can't find me;*
> *If she does, she'll break my bones,*
> *And bury me under the marble stones.'*

But the apple tree said, 'How can I hide you? My branches are trailing on the ground. They will break if you touch them.'

So the girl ran on.

16

Very soon the witch came up, and said:

'*Tree of mine, tree of mine,*
Have you seen a girl,
With a willy-willy wag, and a long-tailed bag,
Who's stolen my money, all I had?'

And the apple tree answered, 'Yes, mother; she's gone down that way.'

So the witch ran, and the girl ran, but the witch ran fastest. Very soon she caught the girl, took all the money away from her, beat her soundly, and sent her home.

So all that girl carried home with her was an aching back.

2 · Rapunzel

Once upon a time a man and his wife lived in a little house that had a window on the stairs looking out over a beautiful garden. The garden had a high wall all round it, and behind the wall every kind of lovely flower grew and flourished. There were fine neat rows of vegetables, too, and trees laden down with all manner of delicious fruit. But no one ever dared to go into the garden, because it belonged to a witch.

Now one hot day the wife was sweeping down the stairs and she felt faint; so she went to the window and opened it, to get a breath of air. She looked down on the witch's garden, and saw a shining green row of rampion, which is a kind of salad.

'Oh,' thought she, 'if I could only have some of that lovely green rampion, I'm sure it would do me good!'

But she knew she couldn't have some of that lovely green rampion; and that made her want it all the more.

Every day after that, she went to the window to look at the rampion. And the more she looked at it, the more she longed for it. So what with worrying about wanting it, and worrying about not being able to have it, she became really ill.

Her husband was troubled to see her looking so wretched.

'Dear wife,' said he, 'what can I do to make you well again?'

'Oh, oh,' said she. 'I've such a longing for some of that rampion, that if I don't get it I shall die!'

'No, no, you shan't die,' said her husband. 'I'll get you some.'

So he waited till dusk, and then he went and climbed over the garden wall, ran to the rampion bed, quickly plucked a big handful of it, scrambled back over the wall, and brought the rampion to his wife.

The wife made a salad of it and ate it. It was delicious. 'Now I am well again,' she said.

But next day she again had a longing for rampion. And as the days passed the longing grew and grew. She wouldn't eat anything, and became ill and wretched.

Her husband said, 'Dear wife, what can I do to make you well again?'

'Oh, oh!' said she. 'If I don't get some more of that rampion, I know I shall die!'

'No, no, you shan't die,' said he. 'I'll get you some more.'

So he waited till dusk, and then climbed over the garden wall for a second time, and ran to the rampion bed.

But the witch was hiding behind a bush, and she pounced out and grabbed him with her bony hand.

'Thief, thief, thief!' she screeched. 'What do I do when I catch a thief? I roast him for dinner!'

The poor man fell on his knees and begged her to forgive him. He told her about his wife, and her longing for the rampion so greatly that if she didn't get it she would surely die.

The witch hummed and hawed and muttered to herself, and then she said, 'Listen to me: I will make a bargain with you. In seven moons from now your wife will have a baby girl. I have never had a baby girl, and I long for one. Promise me that as soon as the baby is born you will give it to me, and in the meantime your wife shall have as much rampion as she likes. But if you do *not* promise to give me the baby, into the oven you go this very night. Now, take your choice!'

What could the poor man do? He promised that if his wife had a baby girl he would give it to the witch. And he went home with two great handfuls of rampion. But he was shaking with grief and fright, and praying that if his wife did have a baby it might be a boy.

But all turned out just as the witch had said. When seven moons were passed his wife had a baby, and it was a girl. And no sooner was the baby born than the witch came scrambling down the chimney, and pounced on it.

The wife cried out in terror, and the witch said, 'Now don't you howl like that! You will have plenty more children; but this baby is my one and only treasure. I have thought of the very name for her, and that is Rapunzel, which means rampion . . . Come along with your new mammy, my sweet little Rapunzel!' And she wrapped the baby in her shawl, and vanished up the chimney with it.

Well, well, the man and his wife never saw Rapunzel again; but as the years passed they did have more children, and that comforted them.

Meanwhile Rapunzel lived with her new mother, the witch, and she was the loveliest little girl that ever the sun shone on. Her eyes shone like stars, and her hair glittered like the sun, and that hair was so long that when she took it out of its plaits it floated behind her in a golden cloud. She had a beautiful voice, too, and sang more sweetly than any nightingale.

The witch doted on her, but she was so furiously jealous that she wouldn't let anyone else come near the child. She looked upon Rapunzel as her greatest treasure, and she was afraid lest someone might steal her treasure from her. And as the years passed, and Rapunzel grew from a lovely child into a beautiful maiden, the witch became more and more worried about how to keep her treasure safe.

So what did that witch do? She shut Rapunzel up in a tall tower in the middle of a wood. The tower had no door and no stairs, and there was no way of getting into it, or out of it, except through a

little window high up under the tower roof. So when the witch wanted to get in, she stood at the bottom of the tower and called out:
>'*Rapunzel, Rapunzel,*
>*Let down your golden hair.*'

Then Rapunzel would take her hair out of its plaits, and shake it down through the window until it reached the ground. And the witch would grasp the golden hair in both hands and climb up by it.

Every day the witch came to pay Rapunzel a visit, but no one else came near her; and when Rapunzel looked out through the tower window, she could see nothing but the tops of the tall trees and the birds that nested in them.

To amuse herself, Rapunzel made up songs about the birds; and when the tower window was open, her beautiful singing floated out and filled the wood with melody. The birds hushed their songs to listen; the deer and the hares and the foxes and the rabbits stood still and pricked their ears at the sound of that singing; and the breezes gathered up the songs and carried them far and wide, whispering to each other, 'How sweet they are! How sweet!'

When the witch heard that singing, and looked up at the height of the tower, she chuckled with delight. 'I have my bird safely caged at last,' she told herself; 'it is not possible for anyone to steal her from me!'

But it so happened that one day when Rapunzel was singing, a prince came riding through the wood; and when he drew near the tower he heard such singing as put the very nightingales to shame. He got off his horse, crept quietly to the foot of the tower, and stood spellbound to listen. And when the song was ended, he sighed and drew his hand across his eyes as if he had just awakened from a dream. He longed to see the owner of that lovely voice; but though he walked all round the tower, he could find no way of getting into it. So he had to ride home again.

All night the prince dreamed of that marvellous singing; and next day he went again to the wood and hid behind a tree. 'Perhaps if she does not see me, she will sing again,' he thought. 'Perhaps, even, she will come to that high up window and I shall see *her* . . . Oh beautiful voice, how beautiful must your owner be!'

Yes, the prince had fallen in love with Rapunzel already, though he had never seen her.

And as he stood there, hidden behind the tree, he heard a crashing in the wood, and the witch came striding to the tower.

> '*Rapunzel, Rapunzel,*
> *Let down your golden hair,*'

she croaked.

The high window opened, two little white hands appeared, and a shower of golden hair fell down to the witch's feet. The witch grabbed the hair and hauled herself up by it. The two little white hands appeared again, the hair went up and up in a golden cloud, and back through the window. The window shut with a slam; and all was silent.

'A golden staircase to my golden love!' said the prince to himself. 'I too will climb that way!'

He waited and waited, hidden behind the tree, till the window opened again. The shower of golden hair fell to the ground once more, the witch came scrambling down it, and went away. And the golden cloud was drawn back up into the tower.

The prince waited and watched and listened. The witch did not come back; twilight fell; all was quiet. He stepped from his hiding place, went to the foot of the tower, and called:

> '*Rapunzel, Rapunzel,*
> *Let down your golden hair.*'

And Rapunzel, who always did what she was told, shook down her hair again: the prince climbed up by it and went in through the window.

When Rapunzel saw him she was frightened, for she had never seen a man before. But the prince knelt at her feet, and spoke to her so very kindly and so very lovingly that she soon forgot her fears. And when he said, 'Rapunzel, will you be my bride?' she answered, 'Yes, I will. I am very lonely here, and I think I should be happier with you. But then – how can I get down from this tower?'

The prince said he would come to visit her every evening, after the witch had gone away; and every evening he would bring with him a skein of silk. Rapunzel should plait this silk into a ladder. When the ladder was long enough she could climb down by it. Then he would put her on his horse, and they would ride away together.

And Rapunzel clapped her hands and said, 'How lovely that will be!'

If Rapunzel's singing had been lovely before, it was even lovelier now that the prince came each evening to visit her. The witch was delighted. 'Talk about giving a bird its freedom!' she cackled. 'The longer you keep it in a cage, the more sweetly it sings! *My* bird has no need to spread its wings!'

And all the time Rapunzel was working away to make a ladder with the silk the prince brought to her; and she was thinking of nothing but of the day when she would escape from her cage and fly away.

All went well for a time. The silken ladder was nearly finished, when one afternoon, as the witch climbed up, she tugged and clawed so at Rapunzel's hair, that Rapunzel exclaimed, 'Oh Mother, you are so heavy, and you do so hurt my head when you tug like that! Why can't you climb up gently like other people?'

'Other people!' screamed the witch. 'What do you mean by "*other people*"?'

Poor Rapunzel! She said she meant nothing, nothing at all. But the witch wouldn't leave it at that; she bullied and screamed and raged and stamped until she had Rapunzel in tears. And then she poked about the room and found the silken ladder hidden under Rapunzel's mattress. And after that – out it came, all about the prince and the ladder and everything.

All the witch's love for Rapunzel now turned to jealous hatred. 'You wicked, wicked girl!' she screamed. 'I'll teach you to deceive me!' And she seized Rapunzel's glittering hair, wound it round and round her left arm, took a big pair of shears in her right hand, and cut off the hair close to Rapunzel's head. After that she began muttering spells till Rapunzel fell down senseless.

When Rapunzel came to herself, the tower had vanished, and the witch had vanished, and Rapunzel found herself in a little hut, far, far away in the middle of a wilderness.

'Oh my prince, my prince,' she wept. 'Now I shall never see you again!'

And far off across the wilderness she heard the old witch laughing.

That evening, the witch fastened Rapunzel's hair to a hook in the tower window. The prince came as usual and called:

> 'Rapunzel, Rapunzel,
> Let down your golden hair.'

The witch shook the hair out of the window; the prince climbed up. But when he came in through the window, there, instead of his lovely Rapunzel, what should he see but the old witch with her eyes glittering with hatred, and her jaws stretched in one huge malicious grin.

'Ha, ha, ha!' she mocked. 'So you have come to visit your pretty little caged bird! But the pretty little bird has flown, and her song is dumb. The cat has caught her. And now the cat will scratch your eyes out!'

24

And she stretched out her bony hand and drew her long nails across the prince's eyes and blinded him.

Beside himself with grief and pain, the prince made a clutch for the golden hair that was still hanging from the window. He leaped out and scrambled part way down, clinging to the hair. But he lost his hold and fell, and if he had not fallen on to a heap of withered leaves, that would have been the end of him. Shaken and bruised and completely blind, he groped his way among the trees, calling and calling, 'Rapunzel, where are you? Oh my Rapunzel, where are you?'

But no voice answered him. He only heard, ringing out from the tower, the cruel laughter of the old witch, 'Ha, ha, ha!' And again, 'Ha, ha, ha!'

So he wandered, blind and miserable, for a whole year, with nothing to eat but berries and roots, and nothing to drink but water from the pools. And at the end of that year he came to the wilderness where Rapunzel was living. Then indeed he heard a voice he knew, a weeping voice that said, 'Oh my prince, my prince, now I shall never see you again!' He groped his way towards the voice. Rapunzel saw him: she ran and took him in her arms, and wept. And two of her tears fell on his blind eyes, and the sight came back to them.

Rapunzel was all in rags, but her glittering hair had grown again; it streamed about her in a golden cloud, making even her rags beautiful. The prince took her by the hand, and they set off together for his father's kingdom. They wandered many a weary mile before they reached it; but reach it they did at last.

They were welcomed by the prince's parents with cries of joy, and lived thereafter all their lives in happiness and peace.

3 · Lazy Hans

Now you must know that there was a widow who had a lazy son. Hans was his name. That lad wouldn't stir a finger to help his mother; he sat in the sun all day, and expected her to feed and clothe him.

Well, when he was a little chap, that was all right; but when he grew into a great strong hulk of a fellow, his mother could stand his ways no longer.

So one day she took a stick to him and said, 'Be off! Earn your own bread and trouble me no more!'

'Oh, all right, if that's how you feel,' said Hans.

And he got up from the grass where he was lying, and leisurely took the road.

He ambled along the road, and he ambled along the road. When he saw nuts in the hedge, he picked and ate them; and when he saw a bright stream at his side, he cupped his hands and drank. When he came to a soft place of moss and fallen leaves, he laid him down and slept.

Thought he, 'What is all this chatter about work? A fellow can live quite well without it!'

All right; so he could, for a bit. But then he came into a barren country – a country where no hedges grew, where no streams flowed, where the pools were brackish, and the ground was covered with prickles.

Thought he, 'I have only to walk on a little farther, and I shall find something different.'

So he walked a little farther, but he didn't find anything different, except that the country became more barren, and yet more barren. And he was hungry and thirsty and desolate-feeling.

Then he came to a little straggly wood, and all the leaves had fallen from the trees and were lying about in yellow withered heaps. He walked through the wood, and a bit of a way farther on was a small stone house, with a great barn at the side of it.

Said he to himself, 'Perhaps whoever lives here will give me something to eat'. And he went and knocked at the door.

Out came an old witch. She squinted at him and said, 'What do you want?'

'Something to eat,' said Hans.

'Something to eat, indeed!' said she. 'If you want something to eat you must work for it.'

'Oh, all right, if that's how you feel, I will work.'

'Mind you, it will be easy work,' said the witch.

'The easier the better,' said Hans.

So she took him in, and gave him a plate of bread and cheese, and some water to drink. 'Now you can go and sleep in the barn,' said she. 'You will start work at dawn tomorrow.'

'Isn't that a bit too early?' said Hans.

'No,' snapped the witch, 'it is not too early. Go to the barn.'

'I would rather sleep by the fire,' said Hans.

'You will sleep in the barn,' said the witch. And she drove him out and bolted the door against him.

There was nothing whatever in the barn. It had a stone floor, and was cold and draughty. There wasn't even a sack or a truss of straw to make Hans a bed. He had a restless night of it, but he fell asleep at last, and woke stiff and cold to find the witch shaking him.

'Surely it's not dawn yet!' he said.

'Dawn indeed!' snapped the witch. 'The sun has risen!'

And, sure enough, when Hans came out of the barn, yawning and rubbing his eyes, a pale ghost of a sun was peering at him over the top of the straggly wood.

He got bread for his breakfast, and a mug of cold water. He asked for cheese, but the witch wouldn't give him any. 'Cheese is for supper when you've done your work,' she said.

Said Hans, 'You needn't snap my head off.'

Said she, 'I'll twist your neck round three times if you don't mind your manners!'

'I think I'll be going,' said Hans.

'You'll not be going till you've earned your night's lodging,' said she. And she laid a spell on the threshold so that Hans couldn't cross it.

'Well then,' said he, 'tell me what I must do. You said it was to be easy work; and if it isn't easy work, you won't find me doing it.'

The witch gave him a heavy stick, as big as himself, and pointed at one end.

'And what am I to do with this?' said Hans.

Said she, 'Three miles from here, if you walk westward, you will come to a field of corn. What you have to do is to plant the stick in the middle of the cornfield.'

'Is that all?' said Hans.

'That's all,' said she.

'Oh ho!' said he, 'I'll soon do that!'

'The sooner the better,' said the witch.

So Hans set out with the stick. He went westward, and the way led him back through the straggly wood. The stick was heavy, and he was feeling stiff and sleepy after his restless night. So, in the middle of the wood he sat down on a heap of yellow leaves.

'There's no hurry. It can't take me all day to walk three miles and back,' he thought. 'So I'll just have a nap before I go on.'

He sat on that pile of leaves, yawning and yawning, and soon he fell asleep. When he woke up it was evening. 'Oh lord!' thought he, 'if I have to walk three miles to that field and three miles back again, I shall be benighted. I won't do it! What's the sense, anyway, of planting a stick in the middle of a cornfield? The old woman's crazy! One place to plant a stick is as good as another – it won't grow wherever it's planted.'

So what did he do but push the point of the stick into a pile of leaves. And he left it standing there, and sauntered back to the witch's house.

'Did you plant the stick as I told you?' said she.

'I did,' said Hans.

'You've taken your time about it,' said she.

'Well, and why not?' said Hans.

She gave him his supper of bread and cheese.

'But I'm not going to bed in that barn again unless you give me something to lie on,' said Hans.

'There'll be plenty to lie on by the morning,' said the witch.

'I'm not talking of the morning, I'm talking of now,' said Hans.

The witch threw him a bundle of sacks; and he took them, went to the barn, rolled himself up in the sacks, and fell asleep. At midnight he was wakened by a rattling at the door that sounded like hail. He went to the door to look out, but it flew open before he reached it, and a cloud of yellow leaves whirled in and hit him in the face.

'Welcome!' said Hans, 'however you've got here! You'll make me a good, soft bed.' And he beat the leaves off with his hands, and began piling them up in a corner. But *swish, hurry, scurry* – in whirled more leaves, and more and more, and they came with such headlong speed that they knocked him backwards. They were up to his knees now, and they were spinning round his head, and hitting him in the face and blinding him.

Hans struggled his way to the door to try and shut it, but the door wouldn't shut, and still a thick cloud of leaves was whirling in from

30

outside. He put his head down and fought his way through them. And when he got through them, what did he see by the light of a waning moon? He saw the witch's stick hopping along on its pointed end, and driving the leaves before it.

When the barn was full to the roof, the stick hopped its way back into the witch's house, and Hans sat down on the doorstep to wait till morning.

At sunrise the witch came out. She was nodding her head and smiling from ear to ear. 'So the barn's full!' she said.

'Full to the roof,' said Hans.

'Then we shan't starve next winter,' said the witch.

She went to the barn and flung open the door. She gave a shriek. 'Leaves!' she screamed, '*Leaves!* What's the meaning of this? Where's the corn? Didn't you plant the stick in the cornfield?'

'I did not,' said Hans. 'I fell asleep in the wood, and when I woke up it was dark. So I planted the stick in the wood and came back. How was I to know what the stick would do?'

'You lazy pig!' screamed the witch.

31

'You needn't call me names,' said Hans.

'It's more than names, it's facts!' she shouted.

And she whipped a large iron ring out of her pocket and tossed it into Hans' face.

What Hans had been going to say, I can't tell you; for all he did say was '*Grumph!*' She had turned him into a pig.

'Since you're so fond of the wood you can go and live in it!' she said. 'And when I've fattened you up, I'll eat you.'

Pig-Hans ran off to the wood. He didn't mean to stay there. He didn't like the idea of being eaten. So he thought he would get out on the far side of the wood and go home. But the witch laid a spell all round the trees, and he couldn't get beyond them. So in the wood he had to stay.

Every morning and every evening the witch came to the wood with a pail of swill for him. But though Hans felt very hungry he scarcely ate any of it. He was too afraid of getting fat and fit to eat. But what Hans left of the swill, and that was most of it, the foxes came and ate up, so that the pail was always empty when the witch came for it.

'Get fat, get fat, get fat!' screamed the witch, poking and pinching him. 'Why don't you get fat?'

But Pig-Hans got thinner and thinner. And at last the witch said, 'Well, if I can't fatten you, I may as well take you for a servant again.' And she pulled the ring out of the pig's nose and turned Hans back into a man.

'Are you going to work for me and obey orders now?' said the witch.

Said Hans, 'If I must, I suppose I must.'

'See you do,' said the witch. And she fetched her stick and told him to go and plant it in a dairy ten miles away, so that it might bring all the milk churns into the barn.

Hans set out. He meant to go and plant that stick where he was told this time. He walked valiantly for five miles, and he walked less valiantly for another three miles; and it seemed to him that the stick got heavier and heavier. He walked on for another mile, but he could scarcely drag one foot behind the other. 'I must just have five minutes rest,' he said to himself. And seeing a large mound by the wayside, he clambered up on to it, thrust the stick upright into the middle of it, lay down, and was soon fast asleep.

When he woke up it was dark. He scrambled to his feet, and felt about for the stick. Well, well, for a long time he couldn't find it anywhere. It had sunk deep down, and there was not more than half an inch of the head of it standing up above the mound. When at last Hans' groping fingers found this half inch, he tried to pull the stick out. But it was wedged tight between two hard pieces of metal, and he couldn't budge it.

He gave up trying at last, and decided to walk away and away into the night, and never go back to the witch's house. And he did walk away, but the witch had put a spell on the road; and the way he had come was the way he must walk back, however much he tried to walk in the opposite direction.

So there he was at last back in the barn; and as before, he was wakened at midnight by a rattling at the door. The door flew open but it wasn't milk churns that the stick was driving in: it was tin cans and pieces of cart wheels, and broken glass and china, and rusty pots and leaky kettles, and bits of bedsteads; for the mound where he had left the stick was an old rubbish dump.

Hans was cut and bruised and battered and scared out of his wits, before he could make his way out through all this rubbish. And still it came pouring in. And behind the rubbish came the stick, hopping along on its pointed end, driving the rubbish before it.

When the barn was full to the roof, the stick hopped its way back into the witch's house, and Hans sat down on the doorstep to wait till morning.

33

At sunrise the witch came out, nodding her head and smiling from ear to ear.

'Did you go to sleep in the wood again?' said she.

'I did not,' said Hans.

'Did you plant the stick as I told you?'

'I did,' said Hans.

'And is the barn full?'

'Full to the roof,' said Hans.

'Ah ha!' said the witch, 'then we shall have plenty of milk!'

She went to the barn, and flung open the door. But when she saw all the rubbish piled up to the roof, she screamed with rage.

'Well,' said Hans, 'I couldn't help it. I fell asleep on the mound and put the stick to stand behind my head. It sank in, and I couldn't pull it out. *I'm* not to blame for the antics it plays.'

'You've no more sense than a gander!' screamed the witch.

'You needn't . . .' began Hans. But whatever he meant to say, all he did was to hiss. For the witch had tied a striped scarf round his neck, and turned him into a gander.

'And don't think starving yourself will do you any good this time,' she yelled, 'for fat or thin, I'll cook you for Christmas!'

Gander-Hans hissed again; he stretched out his neck and pecked at the witch's feet. She gave a jump back, and he gave a run in the opposite direction; the witch hadn't had time to put a spell round the house, so Gander-Hans spread his wings and flew away.

He flew and flew and flew until he came to a wide meadow, where a flock of geese were nibbling at the grass. Then he furled his wings and came down.

'Oh look!' cried the geese, 'look at this queer gander with a scarf round his neck!'

'It's a decoration,' said Gander-Hans, who found he could speak goose-language quite well. 'It was tied round my neck by a queen. No other gander in the world has a decoration like mine!' And he began to waddle about and stretch out his neck. 'You see how the colours glitter when the sun catches them.'

'What did you do to win it?' asked the geese, who were very impressed.

'I brought her all sorts of valuable things,' said Gander-Hans. 'Things she couldn't possibly have obtained otherwise. I went through great perils and dangers to procure them. Oh, I can tell you, I didn't get this decoration for nothing! And now that I have come among you, I expect to be treated with due respect.'

The geese did treat him with respect. In fact, they squabbled as to which of them should feed nearest to him, and he teased them by favouring first one and then another. He nibbled the meadow grass and it tasted good to him; and when he was tired of nibbling the grass, he spread his great white wings and flew to bathe in a nearby lake; and all the geese spread their wings and came after him, pecking and hissing and trying to jostle each other away from his side.

'Ha! Ha! Ha!' laughed Gander-Hans. 'This is a fine life. Plenty to eat, plenty to drink, plenty of admiration – and no work!'

And he lived with the geese for a whole year.

But one day in spring there was a clanging of wings in the air, and a big white bird came flying over the meadow. Another gander! The new gander circled once or twice over the meadow, and then down he swooped and alighted on the grass in the midst of the geese.

'Get out!' hissed Gander-Hans.

'Get out yourself,' hissed the new gander. 'You with a rag round your neck!'

'A decoration, you mean!' said Gander-Hans.

'I said a rag, and I mean a rag,' said the new gander. And he gave a peck at the scarf.

Now to tell the truth the scarf was no longer bright and gay, for it had been bleached by the sun, and frayed by the wind, and soaked so often by the water of the lake that it did indeed look more like a rag than anything else. But Gander-Hans reminded himself that he was really a man and not a bird, and he wasn't going to stand any cheek from a mere gander. So he gave that mere gander a vicious peck; and next minute they were at it, hammer and tongs, with feathers flying, and bills snapping, and the geese standing round in an admiring circle to watch the combat.

Which one of those ganders would have defeated the other, there is no telling; for in the struggle the new gander got his bill firmly wedged in the frayed knot of Gander-Hans' scarf; the knot came undone, the scarf fell off, Gander-Hans immediately vanished, and in his place stood Hans.

The new gander stretched out his neck and hissed. Hans raised his arm and shouted, 'Be off!' The new gander waddled away sideways, stretching his neck out, turning his head over his shoulder, and hissing as he went. The geese followed him. They also were hissing; and suddenly the whole flock rose into the air, and flew away.

'Well – I'll be – blowed!' said Hans.

He lifted his arms, he looked at his hands, he felt his face, he bent his knees, he examined one foot and then the other foot. A man again – and what next? No good now to fill his stomach with grass; no good now to go and float on the water. 'I think I had better go home,' he said to himself.

But where was home?

He set off walking westward, since it was from the west he had come. After walking for some hours, he saw on the horizon to the north the straggly wood near the witch's house. 'I will keep clear of that, at all events,' he said to himself. But it gave him his direction, and he came at last on to the fringes of the barren country where he had suffered hunger and thirst, and after that into the fertile country where he had picked nuts and drunk from pleasant streams. And there in the distance he saw the smoke rising from his mother's cottage.

Then he ran, for it came over him how pleased he was to get home, and how much better it was to be a man than a lazy pig or a senseless gander. So he opened the door of his mother's cottage, and there she was sitting by the fire.

She was secretly overjoyed to see him, for she had been feeling very lonely. But all she said was, 'So you've come again, Hans!'

'Yes, Mother, I've come again. You may not believe it, but I've been a pig, and I've been a gander. And I find it is better to be a man.'

'But a man has to work, Hans!'

'I know that, Mother. And now I will work for you.'

And he did work for his mother, and kept her in comfort from that day on. So she lived happily, and he lived happily, ever after.

4 · The Twins and the Snarling Witch

Once upon a time there was a peasant whose wife died and left him with twin children, a boy and a girl. The man did his best to look after the children; but one day, when he was trying to mend their clothes, he thought, 'A woman knows better about these things than I do; I must take another wife.'

And he took another wife.

For a little while all went well; but then the new wife began to dislike the man's children; and that was because she wanted children of her own, and hadn't any. By and by she got so she couldn't bear the sight of the twins.

'I must get rid of them,' she said to herself. 'And I *will* get rid of them!'

So she went to her husband and said, 'I don't feel very well. I need a rest from so much work. Couldn't we send the twins to stay with my grandmother for a time? She is a woman of refinement, and can teach them many things. When I feel well again, they can come back to us.'

The husband, suspecting nothing, agreed. The stepmother went smiling to the twins.

'You have been such good children,' she said, 'that I am sending you to visit my granny, who lives in a pretty little house in a wood.'

'Shall I help you to pack up our clothes?' asked the little girl.

'Oh no,' said the stepmother, 'you needn't take anything with you. My granny will supply you with everything you need.' And she told them the way they must go, to reach the little house in the wood.

The children set out; and the little girl said to the little boy, 'Why was our stepmother smiling like that, since she doesn't like us? I believe she means us some harm. I think on our way we will go and see our own dear granny – our father's mother – and tell her where our stepmother is sending us.'

So they went to their own grandmother's house, and told her where the stepmother was sending them.

'Oh, oh, oh!' cried the grandmother, 'you poor little motherless children! Your stepmother hasn't got a granny! The house she is sending you to is the house of the snarling witch. She doesn't mean you to come back alive. But be civil and obedient to the witch, and perhaps some help may come.'

She gave the children two loaves of bread, a bottle of milk, a bag of nuts, and a ham; and she kissed them and cried over them and bade them good-bye.

The children walked on and soon came to the wood. There was a thicket of prickly sloe bushes in the wood, and in the midst of this thicket was the hut of the snarling witch. The witch was so big, and the hut was so small, that there wasn't room for the witch inside it. She was lying with her head stuck out of the door. One arm was poking through the window; she had one foot in one corner of the room, and another foot in another corner, and her knees were crooked up and touching the ceiling.

'What do you want?' she snarled, when she saw the children.

The children were terrified. The little girl got behind the little boy, and the little boy's legs were trembling so that he could hardly stand. But they both remembered what their grandmother had said about being civil; and the little girl spoke over her

brother's shoulder, and said, 'Good evening, granny. Our stepmother has sent us to stay with you.'

'And we will do everything we can to serve you,' said the little
boy.

'Humph!' snarled the witch. 'So that's it, is it? If you stay here I
shall give you plenty to do; and if you do well, perhaps I shall
reward you. But if you *don't* do well, I have a big pan handy, and
fried with butter you will make me a tasty supper. Now go to bed.'

'Where shall we sleep, please granny?' said the little girl.

'What a question!' snarled the witch. 'Anywhere you like!
Except in my house. You can't sleep in my house, there isn't any
room, as you can see for yourselves, if you're not blind!' And she

straightened one of her legs and thrust it up the chimney, and waggled her great foot out of the chimney pot.

'Let us run away!' whispered the little boy.

'Oh no, you don't!' snarled the witch. 'Where are your manners? You've come to stay with me, haven't you? If I catch you trying to run away, it's into the pan with you, my beauties! Now, now, don't stand gaping at me! Go to bed.'

The children went to lie down under the sloe bushes. They huddled together to keep warm, and sobbed themselves to sleep.

In the morning the witch came out of her house and drove the little girl into it. She gave her some yarn, and told her to spin it. And she gave the little boy a basket, and bade him fill it with sloes. Then she strode off into the wood.

The little girl sat in the house and cried till her eyes were red. She didn't know how to spin. She was looking at the big pan by the fire and thinking how soon she would be frying in it, when she heard the pattering of hundreds of little feet. Mice were running out of every crack and corner of the hut; and one of them jumped into her lap, and said:

'*Little girl, little girl, why cry your eyes red?*
If you want any help, then give us some bread.'

The little girl crumbled up the loaf her grandmother had given her. The mice ate up every crumb, and then they spun the yarn very neatly with their tails. When that was done, their leader jumped up again into the little girl's lap, and told her that the witch had a cat that was very fond of ham.

'If you give the cat your ham,' said the leader of the mice, 'she will tell you how to escape from the witch.'

The little girl thanked all the mice, and ran out to find the cat. Then she saw her brother standing under the sloe bushes with the empty basket in his hand. He had thought his task would be easy enough, but when he reached up to pick the sloes, the branches jerked themselves away high into the air, and all he was getting was scratches.

'I don't know what to do,' he said.

The little girl tried to comfort him; but she didn't know what to do, either.

Then they heard a rustling overhead; and looking up they saw a great company of squirrels scampering among the branches. And the squirrels said:

'What a sad little boy! But surely he knows
If he gives us some nuts we'll pick him the sloes.'

So the little boy took the bag of nuts his grandmother had given him, and emptied it under the bushes. The squirrels gathered up the nuts and ran off with them to their nests; and then they came back and picked the sloes, and dropped them down into the basket, till the basket was full.

The children thanked the squirrels and carried the basket back to the hut; and there was a big cat curled up by the fire. They stroked her and petted her and gave her the ham their grandmother had given them. And when the cat had eaten it all up and was purring loudly, the little girl said:

'Pussy, dear pussy, tell us how we are to get away from the witch.'

The cat thanked them for the ham, and gave them a comb and a pocket handkerchief.

'When you run and the witch comes after you,' she said, 'throw the comb behind you; and where it falls a dense forest will spring up. It will take the witch a long time to get through that forest. But if she gets through and comes after you again, throw the handkerchief behind you. It will turn into a deep, broad river. Of course I can't say for certain, but I have a feeling that you will get safely home . . . Hush! Not another word! I hear her coming.'

The witch stamped in, knocking off half the roof as she did so; the cat got busy washing herself. The witch saw the basket full of sloes and the bundle of spun yarn. Was she pleased? Not she! But all she said was, 'Since you're so clever, you shall have harder tasks tomorrow. Now go to bed!'

She didn't give the children anything to eat, but they still had one of the loaves their grandmother had given them, and the bottle of milk. They shared the loaf and drank the milk, and went to lie down under the sloe bushes, huddled together to keep warm.

In the morning the witch gave the little girl two lengths of linen to weave before night, and the little boy a pile of logs to cut into chips. Then she went away into the wood.

The cat said, 'Give me that linen to weave; and as for the logs, leave them where they are. Now run off with you – you mayn't get another chance!'

The children said good-bye to the cat, and ran off. The cat called after them, 'Have you got the comb and the handkerchief?'

'Yes, yes, we've got them,' the children shouted back.

They ran and ran and ran. The cat took the linen and began to weave it. But she tangled up all the threads, so that what she wove was quite useless. By and by the witch came tiptoeing to the window.

'Are you weaving, my pretty little dear?' she snarled.

'Yes, granny, I'm weaving,' said the cat.

'Then keep at it, keep at it!' snarled the witch. 'If you don't get it finished before night, the pan is waiting!'

'Oh granny, I'm doing my best!' said the cat.

The witch went away then. But she hadn't gone far when she said to herself, 'Surely that wasn't the little girl's voice!' And she went bounding back to the hut, and wrenched the door open.

When she saw the cat sitting before the loom, and no little girl anywhere, she flung a porringer at the cat and yelled out, 'Why did

43

you let the children escape? Why didn't you scratch their eyes out?'

The cat arched her back and spat.

'I have served you all these years, and you never gave me so much as a fish scale,' she said. 'But the children gave me all their ham.'

The witch threw the frying pan at the cat, and the cat spat again.

'Take care, take care,' said the cat, 'or maybe I shall scratch *your* eyes out.'

'Insolent creature!' snarled the witch. 'I can't stop now, but you shall pay for this when I get back!'

'*If* you get back?' said the cat.

The witch threw a stool at the cat, and then she got astride her broom, and set off in pursuit of the children.

The witch expected the broom to fly through the air, but the broom said, 'I can't fly today. You rode me too hard last night, and I'm stiff all over.'

'I'll soon unstiffen you!' snarled the witch. And she lerruped the broom and lerruped it; and though it didn't fly, it went swishing along the ground at a great rate.

'Faster, faster!' snarled the witch.

But the broom said, 'I can't go any faster. If you lerrup me much more, I shall throw you off!'

The children were running and running. They heard the swish of the broom coming closer and closer. Then the little girl threw the comb behind her, and a great forest sprang up. The branches of the forest were so intertwined that the witch couldn't make her way through them. She had to go home and fetch an axe; and by the time she had hewed her way through the tangle of trees, the children were a long way ahead.

'Faster, faster!' snarled the witch, lerruping the broom.

'I'm going as fast as I can,' said the broom, 'and if you lerrup me much more, you know what will happen.'

'When I get home, I'll chop you up for firewood,' snarled the witch.

'*When* you get home!' mocked the broom.

The children were running and running; but the witch was catching them up. They heard the swishing of the broom. The little boy threw the handkerchief over his shoulder, and in a moment a deep broad river was flowing behind them.

The witch came to the river, and lerruped the broom. 'Fly over it!' she snarled.

'I can't fly,' said the broom.

'You can and you must!' snarled the witch. And she gave the broom such a lerrup that it leaped high into the air. It began to fly over the river, and the witch went on lerruping it. She was mad with rage. The broom said, 'I won't stand any more of this!' So, when they were over the middle of the river, it gave a kick, and the witch fell off with a scream. She fell into the river, and the river carried her away. But where it carried her, no one knows – she was never seen again.

So the broom went back to the hut and lived with the cat, and the children got safely home. They told their father all they had suffered, and he was so angry with the stepmother that he drove her out of his house.

'I must do the best I can for my children without any help,' he said.

And he did his best, and his best was very good. So they all three lived happily ever after.

5 · Esben and the Witch

Once upon a time there was a man who had twelve sons. Eleven of these sons were big, lusty lads; but the twelfth, whose name was Esben, was only a little fellow. The eleven elder brothers despised Esben, and his father thought nothing of him. It was only Esben's mother who had a soft corner for him in her heart. So Esben mostly stayed at home and helped his mother, whilst his eleven brothers worked with their father in the fields.

Now when these eleven sons were grown to be men, they went to their father and said, 'Father, give us each a horse and a sum of money. It is time for us to go out into the world.'

'Oh no, my sons!' said their father. 'I am growing old. Stay with me, that my last years on earth may be free from trouble.'

But no, they would go. They plagued and plagued their father until in the end he had to agree. So they each got from him a fine white horse and a sum of money, and off they went.

When they had gone, Esben said, 'Father, give me also a horse and a sum of money, that I may go out into the world, like my brothers.'

'You are a little fool!' said his father. 'I will give you neither horse nor money. But if I could have kept your brothers at home, and sent *you* away, it would have been better for me in my old age.'

'Well, well,' said Esben, 'I think you will soon be rid of me.'

Since he couldn't get a horse, he went off into the woods and looked among the trees till he found a branch to his liking. And

when he had found a branch to his liking, he cut it down, and chopped it and chipped it into the semblance of a horse, leaving four
strong twigs for its four legs, a knobby end for its head, and a thin
end for its tail. Next, he peeled off the bark and polished the wood
till it shone more whitely than his brothers' horses. And having done
all that, he got astride it, and sang out:

> '*Fly quick, my little stick,*
> *Carry me into the world.*'

And the stick kicked up the four strong twigs that were its four
legs, and galloped away with him after his brothers.

The eleven brothers had been riding gaily along all day; and
toward nightfall they came to a great forest. They rode on through
the forest, and now it was growing dark. So, seeing a house among
the trees, they went to it and knocked at the door.

Out came a frightful old woman, mumbling with her lips, and
peering with her eyes. This old woman was a witch, but the
brothers didn't know it – and why should eleven lusty young men
be afraid of one old woman, however ugly? So they asked if they
might lodge there for the night; and she said 'yes', and let them in.

The witch had thirteen daughters, and though they were not
pretty, they were not so very ugly. They waited on the brothers,
and the witch cooked them a splendid supper. And after they had
supped, they went to bed in a great room, which had twenty-four
beds in it: eleven for the brothers and thirteen for the witch's
daughters.

Now all this time Esben's little stick had been carrying him
along after his brothers. It brought him to the door of the witch's
house, and there Esben dismounted, leaned his stick against the
door-post, and crept quietly into the house. He went upstairs
without anyone seeing him, and hid himself under one of the beds.
And there he waited until midnight.

47

By this time his eleven brothers and the witch's thirteen daughters were all sleeping soundly; and Esben took the nightcaps off his brothers' heads, and the nightcaps off eleven of the witch's daughters; and he put the brothers' nightcaps on the daughters, and the daughters' nightcaps on the brothers. Then he went to hide under the bed again. By and by in came the witch, treading softly as a cat. And she had an axe in her hand. It was so dark that with her bleary old eyes she couldn't see a thing; but she went feeling among the sleepers, and when she felt a man's nightcap she chopped off the head that wore it. And so it came about that she chopped off the heads of eleven of her daughters. And when the eleventh head was off, she crept out again, treading softly as a cat, and well pleased with herself.

And she went to her bed and snored.

As soon as Esben heard the witch snoring he wakened his brothers, and they rose up in terrified haste, escaped from the house, took their horses, and rode off. Did they thank Esben? No, they forgot to do that.

So Esben waited until the sound of their galloping horses dwindled, and then he got astride his little stick, and sang out:

> 'Fly quick, my little stick,
> Carry me after my eleven brothers.'

And the stick kicked up the four twigs that were its four legs, and galloped away with him along the road his brothers had taken.

In the morning the brothers crossed a river and arrived at a king's palace. They asked if they might be taken into service. Yes, they could, if they were content to be stablemen. Otherwise the king had no use for them. So stablemen they became, to look after all the king's horses.

Later in the morning came Esben riding on his little stick. He, too, asked to be taken into service at the palace. But no one had any use for *him* – he was but a little fool, they told him. However, the cook took pity on him and gave him some food. He did little jobs for the cook, and the cook was amused by his comical ways and went on giving him food. So he was able to stay on at the palace. And as to his bed – any odd corner would do for that.

Now there was a knight at the palace called Sir Red, who flattered the king and had won his favour. But he was a bad, cruel man, and, except for the king, everyone hated him. Nevertheless, Sir Red, being the king's favourite, gave himself airs. When he strutted about the palace, or out into the grounds, he expected everyone he met to stand at attention for him; and since Esben's eleven brothers saw no reason why they should do this, Sir Red was furious and determined to ruin them.

So one day he went to the king and said, 'Those new stablemen of yours are cleverer than you think. I overheard them talking this morning, and they said that if they chose they could get you a wonderful dove, which is all covered with gold and silver feathers: one feather gold, the next silver, the next gold, the next silver, and so on, turn and turn about. But they did not choose to go on such an errand, they said, and would not, unless they were threatened with death.'

The king said, 'I would like to possess such a bird!'

Sir Red said, 'Then send for your stablemen.'

The king sent for the brothers and said, 'I hear you have been boasting that you can get me a dove with feathers of gold and feathers of silver.'

The brothers were astonished. All eleven of them declared that they had never said any such thing. Nor did they believe that such a bird existed.

But the king said, 'Take your choice. I give you three days. Bring me the bird, or lose your heads.'

The brothers went back to their work, lamenting bitterly. Esben found them weeping and wailing, and said, 'What's the matter now?'

'Little fool!' said they. 'What good in telling you? *You* can't help us!'

'Oh you don't know that,' said Esben. 'I helped you before.'

So in the end they told him how within three days they must get the king a dove with feathers of gold and feathers of silver. Or, if they did not get it, they must lose their heads.

'So lose our heads we shall,' they wailed. 'For there is no such bird in all the world.'

'Oh you don't know that!' said Esben. 'Give me a bag of peas and perhaps I can help you.'

'Peas, peas, peas!' they cried. 'What good are peas to doomed men? Go away, little fool, and leave us to our misery!'

But Esben wouldn't go away. And at last the brothers gave him a bag of peas to get rid of him.

Esben took the bag of peas, got astride his white stick, and sang out:

> *'Fly quick, my little stick,*
> *Carry me across the stream.'*

Straightaway the stick carried him across the river and into the witch's courtyard; for Esben, whose sharp eyes never missed anything, had noticed that the witch had a dove with alternate gold and silver feathers.

Now he shook the peas out of the bag on to the flagstones of the courtyard, and down fluttered the dove to pick them up. Esben at once caught the dove, put it in the bag, and was astride his stick again before the witch caught sight of him. But just as he was galloping his stick out of the courtyard, the witch saw him, and came running, and shouted after him:

'Is that you, Esben?'

'Ye-e-es!'

'Is it you that have taken my dove?'

'Ye-e-es!'

'Was it you that made me kill my eleven daughters?'

'Ye-e-es!'

'Are you coming again?'

'That may be,' said Esben.

'Then you'll catch it!' shouted the witch.

The stick carried Esben and the dove back to the king's palace. The brothers took the dove to the king. The king was overjoyed to have such a beautiful bird; and in return he gave the brothers both silver and gold. But they never thought of thanking Esben for what he had done for them.

Sir Red was furious. He went to the king and said, 'So, your stablemen have brought you the dove? But that, after all, is not the best they can do. I heard them boasting that they could, if they were so minded, get hold of a boar with tusks of gold and alternate gold and silver bristles.'

The king said, 'I should like to possess such a marvellous boar!' And he sent for the brothers.

Said he, 'I hear you have been boasting that you can get hold of a boar with tusks of gold and alternate gold and silver bristles.'

'No, no!' cried the brothers. 'We never boasted of any such thing. Such a boar does not exist on earth!'

'Take your choice,' said the king. 'Bring me that boar within three days, or lose your heads.'

Off went the brothers lamenting. They sat in the stable among the king's horses, wailing and beating their breasts. Then came Esben to them.

'Hullo! What's the matter here?'

'Oh! Oh! Oh! what's the use of telling a little fool like you? *You* can't help us!'

'Oh, you don't know that,' said Esben. 'I've helped you before.'

So they told him.

And Esben said, 'Give me a sack of malt, and perhaps I can help you.'

They fetched a sack of malt. Esben took the sack, got astride his white stick, and sang out,

'*Fly quick, my little stick,*
Carry me across the stream,'

for he had noticed that the witch possessed such a boar as the king asked for.

Off galloped the stick, over the river and into the witch's court-yard. There Esben emptied the malt out of the bag. Then came the boar with tusks of gold and alternate gold and silver bristles. The boar was snuffing at the malt, but Esben quickly drew the sack over him, and tied it tight. He was astride his stick again with the sack in his arms before the witch caught sight of him. But, as the stick was galloping out of the courtyard, she came running and shouted:

'Hey, is that you, Esben?'

'Ye-e-es!'

'Is it you that have taken my pretty boar?'

'Ye-e-es!'

'Was it you that took my dove?'

'Ye-e-es!'

'Was it you that made me kill my eleven daughters?'

'Ye-e-es!'

'Are you coming back again?'

'That may be,' said Esben.

'Then you'll catch it!' shouted the witch.

The stick carried Esben and the boar back to the king's palace. The brothers took the boar to the king; but again they forgot to thank Esben for what he had done for them.

The king was delighted with his gold and silver boar; he couldn't make enough of the brothers. He raised them from stablemen to equerries, clothed them in fine garments, and heaped gold and silver on them.

And Sir Red raged in his heart. He went to the king and said, 'What those eleven brothers have done for you is nothing to what they can do. I heard them boasting that, if they were so minded, they could get you a lamp that shines over seven kingdoms.'

The king sent for the brothers and said, 'Get me the lamp that shines over seven kingdoms.'

'But no such lamp exists!' cried the brothers.

The king said, 'As you have boasted, so you must do: or lose your heads.'

The brothers went out lamenting. Then came Esben to them and said, 'Hullo! What's the matter this time?'

'Go away, you little fool,' said the brothers. '*You* can't help us!'

'You might at least tell me,' said Esben. 'I've helped you before.'

So at last they told him, and he said, 'Give me a bushel of salt. It is not impossible that I can help you.'

They fetched him a bushel of salt; and he took the salt, got astride his white stick and sang out,

> '*Fly quick, my little stick,*
> *Carry me across the stream,*'

for he had noticed that the witch had a lamp that shone over seven kingdoms.

The stick carried him over the river and into the witch's courtyard. It was now evening. The witch and her two remaining daughters were in bed. Esben got on the roof of the house and climbed down the chimney. He searched everywhere for the lamp, but it was one of the witch's greatest treasures. She had hidden it

53

away, and Esben couldn't find it. So he thought 'I must wait till daylight.' And he crept into the baking oven, which was still warm, intending to sleep there.

He was nearly asleep when he heard the witch calling to one of her daughters, 'I have a powerful hunger on me! Get up, lazy bones, and make me some porridge.'

The daughter got out of bed, lit the fire, and hung a pot filled with water over it.

'Don't put any salt in the porridge!' shouted the witch.

'Neither will I,' said the daughter. She went out into the larder to fetch meal to make the porridge, and Esben slipped out of the oven, and emptied the whole bushel of salt into the pot.

Then he went back into the oven.

The daughter came back, put the meal in the pot, cooked the porridge and carried it up to the witch. The witch tasted it and screamed out, 'You stupid wench! Didn't I say no salt? This muck is as salt as the sea! Go and make me some more!'

'There is no more water in the house,' said the daughter. 'Give me the lamp that shines over seven kingdoms to light me; for I must go to the well.'

'Take it,' said the witch. And she told the daughter where she had hidden the lamp. 'But have a care of it,' she said, 'or you'll catch it!'

So the daughter took the lamp that shone over seven kingdoms, lit it, and went out to the well. And Esben slipped out of the oven and after her. When the daughter got to the well, she set the lamp down on a stone, and stooped over the well to draw up a bucketful of water. Esben gave her a push from behind, she tumbled head first into the well, Esben seized up the lamp, made off with it, and got astride his little white stick.

But the witch heard her daughter screaming and struggling in the well, and she bounded from her bed to pull her out. Then she saw

Esben galloping away with the lamp that shone over seven kingdoms, and she shouted after him:

'Hey! Is that you again, Esben?'

'Ye-e-es!'

'Was it you that took my dove?'

'Ye-e-es!'

'And was it you that stole my pretty boar?'

'Ye-e-es!'

'And was it you that made me kill my eleven daughters?'

'Ye-e-es!'

'And have you now taken my lamp and pushed my twelfth
daughter into the well?'

'Ye-e-es!'

'Are you coming back again?'

'That may be,' said Esben.

'Then you'll catch it!' shouted the witch.

So Esben took the lamp to his brothers, and his brothers took it
to the king. The king was a proud man now: the lamp lit up his
whole kingdom, and six other kingdoms as well. He loaded the
brothers with gifts and honours; but Esben did not get so much as
a word of thanks from them.

It was Sir Red who had to stand at attention now, when the
brothers walked past him with their noses in the air. He was eaten
up with jealousy. He couldn't sleep for scheming how to avenge
himself.

One day he went to the king and said, 'All that the brothers have
done is nothing to what they can do. They are boasting now that
they know of a coverlet, hung with golden bells. And this coverlet
is so made that if anyone touches it, the bells give out a ring that
can be heard over eight kingdoms.'

The king said, 'I would like to possess such a coverlet!' And he
sent for the brothers.

Said he, 'You have boasted that you know of a coverlet hung with golden bells whose ring can be heard over eight kingdoms. Get me that coverlet.'

'We cannot get it!' they cried. 'Such a coverlet does not exist on earth!'

'Then you can lose your heads,' said the king.

The brothers went from the king, wailing and lamenting. Then came Esben and said, 'Hullo! What's the matter now?'

'Little fool!' said they. 'You can't even keep yourself in clothes! How can *you* help us?'

'Oh, I don't know that!' said Esben. 'I have helped you before.'

So then they told him about the coverlet. And Esben thought that to get that coverlet would be the very worst errand he had ever set out on, for the coverlet was on the witch's bed. However he could not do worse than fail. So he got astride his white stick, and sang out:

'Fly quick, my little stick,
Carry me across the stream!'

The stick galloped with him across the river and into the witch's courtyard. It was now night. Esben got on to the roof, climbed down the chimney, and crept into the room where the witch was sleeping with the coverlet spread over her. But as soon as he touched the coverlet, the bells gave out a ring that could be heard over eight kingdoms; and the witch bounded up wide awake and caught Esben by the leg.

Esben kicked and struggled. The witch held on to his leg and bawled to her thirteenth daughter, 'Come and help me!' The daughter ran in; they had Esben fast between them; they took him and locked him up in a dark room.

'Now we will fatten him up,' said the witch. 'And when he is fat enough we will eat him.'

It was the thirteenth daughter's task to carry food to Esben, for the twelfth daughter was ill in bed from the fright and the sousing she had got when Esben pushed her into the well. The thirteenth daughter fed Esben on cream and nut kernels. She was kept busy cracking the nuts for him.

'I am breaking every tooth in my head for you,' she said. 'But I don't mind. You are a brave little fellow, and I have come to like you.'

'Then you don't want me to be cooked and eaten?' said Esben.

'No, I do not,' said she. 'But what can I do?'

One day the witch bade this thirteenth daughter to chop off one of Esben's fingers and bring it to her, that she might see whether he was fattening. The daughter came to Esben and said, 'I don't want to chop off your finger!'

So Esben told her to take an iron nail and wrap a bit of silk round it, and take that to the witch, who, like all witches, was dim-sighted.

The witch bit on the nail and said, 'Ugh! Skinny little beggar! Fatten him up, girl, fatten him up!'

So the daughter took Esben more and more food; and some of it he ate, but most she ate. And Esben got weary of sitting in the dark having nothing to do but eat, and he said, 'Let's make an end of it!'

He bade the daughter bring him some fat and a piece of skin, and he rolled the fat up in the skin in the shape of a finger, and said, 'Take that to your mother.'

The witch bit on the false finger. 'Ah ha!' she cried. 'Now he is fat – so fat that one cannot feel a bone in him! He is ready to be roasted!'

Now it happened that this was the very time when all the witches sailed off on their broomsticks for their yearly gathering on a hill called The Hill of Meeting. If any one of the witches missed this gathering, she was sorely punished by the others, so the witch had to go. Before she went she said to her thirteenth daughter,

'Heat the oven and have Esben ready roasted by the time I come back. See that he is neither overdone nor underdone. If you don't cook him nicely, you'll catch it!'

And she got on her broomstick and off she flew.

The daughter went sniffling and snuffling to Esben, and said, 'Oh what a pity, what a pity! Now I've got to roast you!'

Said Esben, 'If you have to roast me, you have to. Let's get it over!'

So the thirteenth daughter let Esben out of the dark room. And when they were both outside the room, Esben said, 'Oh, I've left my hat in there! I won't be roasted without my hat on my head. You go in and get it for me.'

The thirteenth daughter went back into the dark room; Esben locked the door on her, and left her there. He ran up to the witch's bedroom, seized the coverlet and fled with it into the courtyard, where his little stick was propped against the wall. He got astride the stick and sang out:

> 'Fly quick, my little stick,
> Carry me to the king's palace.'

But the coverlet, as soon as Esben touched it, had given out a ring that could be heard over eight kingdoms. The witch, on her way to The Hill of Meeting, heard the ring, and came flying back home on her broomstick. Her thirteenth daughter was banging on the locked door of the dark room and shouting, 'Let me out!' But the witch paid no attention to *her*! She saw Esben galloping out of the courtyard on his little stick, and she rushed after him, shouting:

'Hey! Is that you again, Esben?'

'Ye-e-es!'

'Is it you that made me kill my eleven daughters?'

'Ye-e-es!'

'And took my dove?'

'Ye-e-es!'

'And my pretty boar?'

'Ye-e-es!'

'And pushed my twelfth daughter into the well, and took my lamp?'

'Ye-e-es!'

'And have now locked my thirteenth daughter in the dark room, and stolen my coverlet?'

'Ye-e-es!'

'Are you coming back again?'

'No, never again,' said Esben.

When she heard that, the witch became so furious that she burst into millions of pieces of flint. The flints strewed the country far and wide, as you can see to this day.

When Esben got back to the king's palace, he found his brothers in a bad way. They had all been thrown into prison, and were going to have their heads cut off on the very next morning, because they had not been able to get the coverlet. But Esben gave the coverlet to the king. The king touched the coverlet, and it gave a ring that could be heard over eight kingdoms. He was happy as could be, thinking how jealous the seven kings of the seven other kingdoms must be feeling. So he let the brothers out of prison. And the brothers at last remembered to thank Esben for all he had done for them.

Then Esben told the king the whole story, and the king ordered Sir Red to be whipped and driven out of the country. And he offered dukedoms to all twelve of the brothers.

But the brothers whispered amongst themselves, and said, 'Truly with such a king it is dukedoms today; but as like as not it will be heads off tomorrow!' And they told the king they would rather go home.

The king, who was chuckling with delight over his dove, and his boar and his lamp and his coverlet, said, 'Let everyone do as he pleases!' And he gave the brothers as much gold and silver as they could carry to take home with them. So they mounted on their fine white horses, and Esben followed after them on his little white stick, and they all rode back to their parents.

When the father saw his twelve sons coming, he wept for joy. He had never expected to see them again. The brothers now could not make enough of Esben. They told their father how he had five times saved their lives.

The father said, 'So the fool of the family has turned out the best man of you after all!'

And the mother said, 'Didn't I always know it!'

And they rejoiced and held Esben in great esteem ever after.

6 · Prunella

Once upon a time a little girl was walking along a lane, and she saw a tree covered with ripe red plums. She reached up to pick a plum, and out from behind the tree bounced a witch.

'Ha!' said the witch. 'I've been looking for a little maid like you to keep my house tidy.' And she dragged the little girl over the hedge and into her house.

The house was a queer one. It was built entirely of plum stones; and the chairs and tables and beds were made of plum stones also. The witch called the little girl Prunella, which means 'little plum', and she gave her nothing but plums to eat: five plums for breakfast, ten plums for dinner, and six plums for supper.

'And see that you save all the plum stones carefully,' said the witch, 'because I want to build a porch.'

Prunella often tried to run away. But there was magic all round the place. So that whichever way Prunella began to run, and however far she went, she always found herself, at the end of her running, going in through the witch's front door. And then the witch would shriek with laughter and say, 'When I have a little maid I like to keep her.'

Prunella lived with the witch for years and years. And strange to say, though she got nothing but plums to eat, she was always well and strong, and she grew prettier and prettier. By the time she was seventeen years old you couldn't have found a more beautiful girl, had you searched the wide world through.

There was no looking-glass in the witch's house, so that Prunella didn't know how beautiful she was, until one bright day, when she went with her pitcher to the well, she looked down and saw her reflection in the still water.

'Oh!' said Prunella, 'is that really me?'

And she stayed so long by the well, smiling at the pretty image of herself, that the witch came to the door and screamed at her to know what she was doing.

Said Prunella, 'I am looking at myself in the water. I did not know that anyone could be so pretty.'

Said the witch, 'Pretty, pretty! What do you mean? You are just like other people.'

'No,' said Prunella, 'I am not in the least like you. Come and look!'

The witch came bustling to the well; she looked down and saw Prunella's image. She saw, too, her own image, with its great hooked beak of a nose, little red eyes, and craggy chin where a beard sprouted. The contrast was too much; the witch gave Prunella a cuff and sent her crying back into the house. Then she stood by the well, muttering to herself:

'Ho! So you're not in the least like me? I'll teach you to set yourself up above your betters, you vain hussy!'

She stamped into the house again, and gave Prunella a basket.

'Since you think so much of yourself,' she said, 'take this basket to the well and fill it with water. If you don't bring it back full, I will kill you!'

Prunella took the basket and went to the well. She tied a rope to the handle and let the basket down into the well. She let it down again and again; but every time she drew the basket up, the water poured out of it. So at last she gave up trying, and sat down by the well and cried bitterly.

'Prunella, why are you crying?' said a voice.

Prunella looked up, and there, standing at her side, was a splendidly handsome youth.

'Why, who are *you*?' said Prunella. 'Where have you come from, and how do you know my name?'

'I am the son of the witch,' said the youth. 'My name is Benvenuto. I have watched you for a long time. You are beautiful and good, and I love you, Prunella. Give me a kiss, and I will fill your basket for you.'

But Prunella tossed her head, and said, 'I will not kiss the son of a witch.'

'No, I suppose you will not,' said Benvenuto sadly. 'But I will fill your basket for you all the same.' And he took the basket, lowered it into the well, and brought it up full of water.

Prunella carried the basket back to the witch. When the witch saw that it was full of water, she became green with rage, and shrieked out, 'Who filled it?'

'*You* did not, at any rate,' said Prunella.

The witch screamed, 'You have been talking to Benvenuto!'

And Prunella said scornfully, 'Who is Benvenuto that I should talk to him?'

'Well, we shall see who will win in the end,' shouted the witch. 'But I won't stay in the house to have you smirking at me! I am going out for exactly an hour. Here, take this sack of wheat. By the time I come back I shall expect you to have ground the wheat and made all the flour into nice crusty loaves. If you cannot do that, you are no good, and I will kill you.'

The witch locked Prunella in the kitchen and rushed out of the house. Prunella began to grind the flour. She ground and ground, and all the time she was watching the hands of the clock, and the hands of the clock seemed to be racing. Soon fifty-five minutes had gone by, and still the flour was not all ground. In five more minutes the witch would be back. And how could Prunella finish grinding the flour, and prepare the dough, and bake the bread, all in five minutes?

'I can't do it!' she cried. And she threw herself down in a chair, and wept bitterly.

And then she saw Benvenuto standing at her side. And he said, 'Prunella, do not weep like that! If you will give me but one kiss, I will make the bread. And you will be saved.'

But Prunella tossed her head, and said, 'If I must die, I will die. I will not kiss the son of a witch.'

Benvenuto sighed. 'I will help you all the same,' he said. He took the wheat in his hands, and the wheat was flour; he took the flour in his hands, and the flour was dough; he took the dough in his hands, and the dough turned into crusty well-baked loaves all hot from the oven.

Then, as he had come, so he went. The clock struck the hour, the witch unlocked the door, and came bouncing into the kitchen.

When the witch saw the hot crusty loaves, neatly arranged on the table, she turned white and green and yellow with rage. 'Who has done this?' she screamed.

'*You* have not, at any rate,' said Prunella.

The witch shrieked, 'Benvenuto has helped you!'

And Prunella answered scornfully, 'Who is Benvenuto that he should help me?'

The witch's little red eyes were sending out sparks of rage. 'We shall see who will win in the end,' she muttered.

The witch muttered to herself all that day. And all night long she was tossing and turning, thinking how she would get the better of Prunella. At dawn she thought of something, and she bounced out of bed and roused Prunella. She was smiling now, and trying to look pleasant.

'Well, my girl, I see that you are too clever for me,' she said. 'And I have a hasty temper, I must admit. So we will let bygones be bygones, and see if we can't live pleasantly together. Today I am going to send you on a little errand – a change of scene will do you good. You see that mountain over there?'

'Yes,' said Prunella, 'I see it.'

'My sister lives on the other side of that mountain,' said the witch. 'She has a casket of jewels belonging to me, and I want you to go and fetch it. There is a pretty little string of pearls in it, I seem to remember. I fancy they would look well round your white neck. If your do your errand successfully, I will give you that string of pearls. So away you go! . . . Take your time,' said the witch with a giggle. 'On such a beautiful day there's no need to hurry.'

And she thought to herself, 'Prunella will never come back from that errand alive.'

Prunella set out happily. She was glad to get away from the witch's house for a day, and she suspected nothing.

66

'The old thing is in a good temper for once!' she thought; and she went on her way singing to herself. She crossed some fields and she crossed a moor, and came to the foot of the mountain.

And there, at the foot of the mountain, stood Benvenuto.

'Prunella, Prunella, where are you going?'

'I am going to the house of my mistress's sister, to fetch a casket.'

'Oh, you poor girl, you are going to your death!' cried Benvenuto. 'But give me just one kiss, and I will save you!'

Prunella tossed her head. 'If I am going to my death, then I go to my death. I will not kiss the son of a witch.'

Benvenuto sighed and said, 'I cannot let you die! Listen to me. My mother's sister is a witch also, and she is more cruel and wicked even than my mother. She kills everything she can get her hands on, and spares no living creature. But if you do what I tell you, you will escape her. Take this flagon of oil, this loaf of bread, this piece of rope, and this broom. When you come to the sister-witch's courtyard, oil the hinges of the gate, and the gate will let you through. In the courtyard a huge dog will spring out upon you. But throw him the bread and he will let you pass. Then you will come to a well, and you will see a woman trying to draw up buckets of water with her hair. Give her the rope; but do not stay to listen to her thanks. Beyond the well is the door into the kitchen. In the kitchen you will find a woman trying to clean the hearth with her tongue. Give her the broom. The casket is on top of a cupboard. Take it, and run from the house with your utmost speed. If you do all this exactly as I tell you, you will come back safely.'

When he had said this, Benvenuto disappeared, and Prunella went on her way up the mountain. She came to the sister-witch's house, which was surrounded by a large courtyard. The gate into the courtyard was very rusty, but when Prunella emptied the flagon of oil over its hinges, it swung open of its own accord, and she went through.

67

Then a huge black dog came leaping and growling, as if he would tear her to pieces, but she threw him the loaf of bread, and he wagged his tail and let her pass. She crossed the courtyard and came to the well, where she saw a wretched woman trying to draw up water by her long hair, which she had tied to the handle of a bucket. Prunella flung her the rope, and hurried on.

She came to the kitchen door, pushed it open, and went in. And there, crouched before the fire, was another wretched woman, trying to clean the hearth with her tongue. Prunella tossed her the broom, snatched the casket from the top of the cupboard, and ran out again.

But in her hurry she had slammed the kitchen door, and the sister-witch looked out of her bedroom window, and saw Prunella running across the courtyard.

'Hearth-woman, hearth-woman!' shrieked the sister-witch from the top of the stairs. 'Kill that thief!'

But the hearth-woman said, 'No, I will not kill her, for she has given me a broom, whereas you forced me to clean the hearth with my tongue.'

'Well-woman, well-woman!' shrieked the sister-witch from the doorway. 'Drown that thief!'

But the well-woman answered, 'No, I will not drown her, for she has given me a rope, whereas you forced me to use my hair to draw up water.'

'Dog, dog!' shrieked the sister-witch. 'Seize that thief!'

But the dog answered, 'No, I will not seize her, for she gave me a loaf of bread, whereas you left me to starve.'

'Gate, gate!' shrieked the sister-witch, running across the courtyard. 'Bang on that thief, keep her a prisoner!'

But the gate answered, 'No, I will not bang on her; I will let her through, for she oiled my hinges, whereas you left me to rust.'

The gate swung open, and Prunella ran through; the gate

banged shut again, just as the sister-witch reached it. Do what she would, she could not open it again.

And so Prunella got safely back with the casket.

The witch, her mistress, turned first yellow, and then blue, and then purple with anger. 'You did not get that casket yourself,' she screamed. 'Benvenuto gave it to you!'

But Prunella answered scornfully, 'What is Benvenuto to me, or I to him, that he should give me anything?'

'We shall see who will win in the end,' cried the witch, dancing with rage. 'There are three cocks in the hen-house. One is yellow, one is black, and one is white. Tonight, when one of these cocks crows, you must tell me which it is. If you make one mistake, you will never make another, for I will eat you up in a single mouthful.'

Prunella went to her bed, the witch went to hers. At midnight a cock crew.

'Which cock was that?' shouted the witch.

'Oh Benvenuto, Benvenuto!' whispered Prunella. 'If you can hear me, tell me which cock it was that crowed.'

And Benvenuto's voice whispered back, 'Give me a kiss, and I will tell you.'

But Prunella said, 'I will not kiss the son of a witch.'

'Nevertheless,' sighed the voice, 'I will tell you. It was the yellow cock that crowed.'

'Answer me, girl, answer me!' shouted the witch. 'If you don't I will kill you!'

And Prunella answered, 'It was the yellow cock that crowed.'

The witch was so angry that she bounded out of bed and rushed into Prunella's room. 'It was Benvenuto who told you that!' she screamed. 'Where is he?'

And Prunella answered scornfully, 'What is Benvenuto to me, that I should know where he is?'

So the witch went back to bed.

69

By and by a cock crowed again.

'Which cock was that?' shouted the witch.

'Which?' whispered Prunella.

'Give me a kiss, and I will tell you.'

'I cannot kiss the son of a witch.'

'Nevertheless I will tell you,' sighed the voice. 'It was the black cock.'

'Answer me, girl!' shouted the witch.

'It was the black cock,' said Prunella.

The witch was gnashing her teeth. She bit a hole in the sheet; she tore the bedclothes to shreds in her rage. Again a cock crowed, and again the witch shouted, 'Which cock was that?'

'Oh Benvenuto,' whispered Prunella, 'help me yet once again!'

But the voice whispered back, 'I will not help you again unless you kiss me.'

'How can I kiss the son of a witch?' moaned Prunella.

And all the answer she got was a sigh.

'Answer me, girl, answer me!' shouted the witch. 'Which cock was it?'

'I do not know,' whimpered Prunella.

'Then I will kill you!' screamed the witch. And she rushed into Prunella's room.

'Benvenuto! Benvenuto!' cried Prunella. 'Save me!'

In her fright, she ran to the window and leaped out. But she did not fall to the ground. Invisible arms caught her, and a voice said, 'I love you, Prunella. I do not ask anything of you, except to be allowed to save you.'

The invisible arms carried her away and away. The voice whispered and sighed. It was dark, dark night. Prunella thought she heard the roaring of the sea: and then she fell asleep. When she woke up, she was lying on a daisied bank, the sun was shining, the birds were singing, and Benvenuto was standing at her side.

70

'I have put the sea between you and the witch,' he said. 'You are safe now. Good-bye, Prunella.'

He began to walk sadly away, and it seemed to Prunella that he took the daylight with him. She jumped to her feet.

'Benvenuto!' she cried, 'don't leave me! What shall I do alone in the world? What shall I do without you?'

He came back then, and Prunella said, 'Stay with me, I will give you as many kisses as you like.'

'Have you forgotten that I am the son of a witch?' he said.

'Yes,' said Prunella. 'I have forgotten it. I remember only that you are good and kind.'

'And you will be my wife, Prunella?'

'Yes,' said Prunella, 'I will be your wife.'

So they went on their way, and got married, and lived happily ever after.

7 · The Donkey Lettuce

Once upon a time a young hunter was walking through a wood, whistling merrily. And there a poor old woman met him who said, 'Good morning, dear hunter! How happy and contented you seem to be! But as for me, I am poor and hungry and homeless. Can you not spare me a trifle to buy me some food and a night's lodging?'

'Truly, mother, I have not much money about me,' said the hunter. 'But you are welcome to what I have.'

He put his hand in his pocket and brought out a few coins.

'There,' said he, 'take these. I wish for your sake there were more of them.'

And he made to go on his way.

'Stop, stop a little minute!' said the old woman. 'Because of your kind heart I will make you a present. Walk on by this path to the left, and very soon you will come to a tree on which nine birds will be sitting, quarrelling over a cloak which they hold in their claws. Take aim with your gun and shoot up into the midst of them. They will let the cloak fall, and one of the birds will drop down dead. Pick up the cloak and keep it carefully – it is a wishing cloak. You have only to throw it over your shoulders and it will carry you to any place where you may wish to go. Don't overlook the dead bird, either. Cut it open, take out its heart and swallow it; and every morning when you wake you will find a gold coin under your pillow.'

The hunter thanked the old woman and went on his way.

'Well, well,' thought he, 'if she was a fairy, I am in luck, for these are splendid things she has promised me! But like as not it is only an old woman's nonsense. However, here's a path to the left, so let us go down it!'

He had not gone far down that path to the left when he heard a great screeching and clamour over his head. He looked up and saw nine birds among the branches of an elm tree. They had a cloak between them, and they were tearing at it with their beaks and claws, and flapping their wings as if each wanted to snatch the cloak for himself and fly away with it.

'Oh ho!' thought the hunter, 'this is just as the old woman said!' And he put his gun to his shoulder, pulled the trigger, and shot up among the birds. Eight of the birds flew away screaming, but the ninth fell dead at the hunter's feet, and the cloak fluttered to the ground beside it.

'So far so good!' thought the hunter. 'What do we do next? Why, of course, we swallow this fellow's heart, and see what comes of *that*!'

So he cut the bird open, took out its heart and swallowed it. Then he put on the cloak and wished himself at home – and there he was.

Next morning when he looked under his pillow – yes, sure enough, there was a gold piece! And every morning when he woke there was another, and another, and another; until, as weeks went by, he had a neat little hoard of gold. This hoard he gave to his parents, saying, 'You have fed me and clothed me for many years; now here is the wherewithal to feed and clothe *you*. As for me, I think of journeying forth to have a look at the great world.'

He bade good-bye to his parents and set out with a merry heart, whistling and singing as he went. Something of the great world he did see, to be sure, but nothing that particularly took his fancy, until one day as he was crossing a great plain he came to a

73

magnificent castle. At one of the windows an old woman was looking out, and beside the old woman stood a very beautiful girl.

'Oh!' thought the hunter, '*Oh!*' And there he was, standing like
one moonstruck, staring at the girl, until he remembered his
manners, swept off his hat, and made a low bow.

Now the old woman was a witch, and when she saw the hunter,
she said to the girl, 'Here comes one who has a wonderful treasure
in his body! We must get hold of it, daughter dear! We have more
need of it than he has. He has swallowed a bird's heart, and every
morning he finds a piece of gold under his pillow.'

The girl said, 'Let him be.'

The witch said, 'No, we will *not* let him be! If you do as I tell
you, the treasure is ours. If you do not do as I tell you, I will beat
you till I break every bone in your body. Now, go down and bid
him welcome.'

The girl went down unwillingly, and invited the hunter to come
in and rest. He needed no pressing! He followed the girl into the
castle like one in a dream; for he felt that here in this girl was the
beginning and end of all his seeing of the world. The old witch
received him graciously, and fed and housed him sumptuously;
and the silly fellow sat looking into the girl's eyes, and never
thought of why or wherefore, or gave heed to the passing of the
days.

Before the week was out he had asked the girl to be his wife, and
she had consented, for she felt that she loved him truly. But she
dared not disobey her mother; and one evening the witch took her
aside and said to her, 'The time has come for us to have that
heart out of him.'

'Oh no, not yet!' said the girl.

The witch stamped her foot and said, '*Now*, I tell you, *now*! If you
dare to thwart me, I will put serpents in your bed, and there will be
nothing left of you in the morning!'

The girl was frightened and said, 'I will do as you wish.'

The witch then prepared a drink; and when it was ready she poured it into a goblet and gave it to the girl, bidding her hand it to the hunter. She told her what to do and what to say. And the girl took the goblet to the hunter.

'Drink to me, my dearest,' she said.

The hunter took the goblet and drank. As soon as he had swallowed the draught, the bird's heart fell out of his mouth. But he was looking into the girl's eyes and did not notice it. The girl caught the heart in her hand, and swallowed it.

Every morning after that, the girl found a piece of gold under her pillow, and the hunter found none. But the silly fellow was too much in love to heed whether he found any or not. And the witch grabbed the gold and soon had a fine hoard.

One day the witch said to her daughter, 'We have the bird's heart, but we must also get the wishing cloak from him.'

'Oh no!' said the girl. 'We have stolen his wealth – let him keep the cloak!'

'If you do not agree to do as I wish,' screamed the witch, 'I will turn you into a sow, and your hunter shall eat roast pork for dinner!'

So then the girl said, 'I will do as you wish.'

The girl went to stand at a window, and the tears were running out of her eyes.

The hunter came and said, 'Beloved, why do you weep?'

She would have said, 'I weep for the wickedness of my mother', but she dare not. So what she did say was, 'Oh, I am looking at that granite mountain yonder. Do you know that there is a dell up there filled with the most beautiful jewels in the world? I have so great a longing to possess some of those jewels that I cannot help but weep. For no man can climb that mountain. Only the birds can go there.'

75

'Is *that* all your trouble?' cried the hunter. And he wrapped the girl in the folds of his cloak and wished himself at the dell of precious stones in the granite mountain. On the instant, there they were, he and the girl, sitting side by side in the dell, with the precious stones glittering all about them.

'Fill up your apron!' cried the hunter, 'and I will fill my pockets for you!'

And they gathered up some of the most precious of the stones.

But the witch had put a spell on the hunter to make his eyes heavy, and by and by he said, 'I don't know how it is, but I am so sleepy that I can hardly stand on my feet. Let us now sit down and rest for a little while.'

They sat down; the hunter laid his head in the girl's lap, and immediately fell asleep. She shook him once, but he did not waken. She shook him twice – he did not waken. She shook him a third time, and still he slept on. Then she wept and said, 'Now all is over between us!' And she unloosed the cloak from his shoulders, wrapped it round herself, and wished herself back at home.

When the hunter woke, there he found himself, deserted and alone on the great granite mountain. Now he knew that the girl had deceived him, and he cried out, 'Oh my love, my love! Oh what great wickedness there is in the world!' He covered his face with his hands and lay there utterly wretched, sick at heart and not knowing what to do.

Now the mountain belonged to three mighty giants, who lived on it and traded in precious stones. And the hunter had not lain long before he felt the mountain shake under him; and glancing up between his fingers he saw the three giants come striding towards him. There was no time to flee, so he lay very still, as if he were asleep.

The giants came up. The first one pushed the hunter with his great foot, and said, 'What sort of an earthworm is this?'

'Stamp on it!' said the second giant.

But the third giant said, 'It's not worth the trouble of messing your boots. Let him be. He cannot live here. And if he goes higher up the mountain the clouds will carry him away.'

The giants strode off. When they were out of sight, the hunter got up and climbed to the top of the mountain. He waited there till a great white cloud came drifting by. Then he held out his arms. The cloud wound itself around him and lifted him up; and after drifting with him here and there about the sky, it sank down and dropped him gently into a large garden.

The hunter got to his feet and looked about him. He was very hungry; but there were no fruits of any kind in the garden – no nuts or apples or pears or plums; only vegetables and herbs. So he went to a large bed of lettuces. 'Not very appetizing,' said he, 'but better than nothing!' And he picked a lettuce and began to eat it.

Heavens! What was happening to him? His ears were growing long, his arms were turning into legs, his clothes were changing into thick grey fur. He looked at his hands – yes, they were hoofs! He turned his head and glanced over his back – yes, he had a tail! He had turned into a donkey!

He tried to whistle to keep up his spirits. But all the sound that came from his lips was '*Hee-haw-aw-aw-aw!*'

Ah well, there was one good thing about it – the lettuces and the cabbages and the cauliflowers now tasted delicious to him, and he ate and ate, and still he ate, wandering about from one bed to another. Under the garden wall he found another bed of lettuce, of a different shape and flavour from those in the first bed; and these tasted so good that he munched them and munched them – and only stopped munching when he suddenly realized that he had changed back into a man.

'Blessed be the fate that brought me here!' he said aloud. 'For now I know what to do. But first I will sleep.'

77

So he lay down between the vegetable rows and slept.

When he woke in the morning he picked the choicest lettuce he could see from the first bed, and the choicest lettuce he could see from the second bed. 'Now my little vegetables,' he said, 'you shall help me to recover my property and to punish the unfaithful.'

He put the two lettuces in his wallet, climbed over the garden wall, and set out to search for the witch's castle. And after two days' walking, he saw the castle in the distance.

He didn't go at once to the castle. First he went into a wood, plucked some berries, and stained his face and his hands brown. He took out a knife and cut his fair curly hair very short, and that too, he stained brown. Now even his mother would not have known him. He walked boldly on till he came to the castle gate, and there he knocked.

The witch opened the gate and he asked for a night's lodging. 'I am so exhausted,' he said, 'I can't walk another step.'

Said the witch, 'Well, my fine countryman, who are you, and what is your business?'

Said he, 'I am one of the king's messengers, and I have been sent to seek the finest salad that grows under the sun. I have been lucky enough to find it, and am carrying it back to the king. I have it here in my wallet.'

'Friend countryman, you make my mouth water!' said the witch, who was very greedy. 'If I give you a night's lodging, will you not let me taste this wonderful salad?'

'Why not?' said the hunter. 'I have brought two heads of the lettuce with me. I will give you one.'

He opened his knapsack. And what did he do? Why, of course, he gave the witch the donkey lettuce.

'I will prepare it myself,' said the witch. 'I will make a beautiful salad. And you shall have a taste of it, my good countryman.'

But the hunter said, 'I do not care for salad, it does not agree with me.'

'Then there will be all the more for me,' thought the greedy witch; and off she went into the kitchen. She made her salad, putting the lettuce leaves in a dish, and adding hard-boiled eggs and cucumber and radishes. When it was ready, the salad certainly looked very inviting. The witch couldn't wait to have it served at table: she must just taste it. She picked up two of the lettuce leaves and crammed them into her mouth. 'Um, um, um – delicious!'

But – well, there, as soon as she had swallowed those two leaves she turned into a donkey, and ran out braying into the courtyard.

Meanwhile, the hunter had gone upstairs to the dining-room, to talk to the witch's daughter. For, despite all she had done, he was still in love with her – he could not help it. The girl asked what her mother was doing, and the hunter told her that she was in the kitchen, making a salad. So, as the salad did not appear, the girl sent a maid servant down to the kitchen, to see if it was ready.

'Oh, what a beautiful salad!' thought the maid servant, as soon as she saw it. 'I must just taste it!' And she picked up a leaf and ate it. 'Um, um, um – delicious!' But no sooner had the maid servant swallowed that leaf than she turned into a donkey, and ran out braying to join her mistress in the courtyard.

'Are they never going to bring up that salad?' said the girl to the hunter.

'I will go and see about it,' said the hunter.

He went downstairs, looked out of the kitchen window, and saw two donkeys running round the courtyard. 'Ah ha!' thought he, 'two have had their share. Now it is your turn, my fair lady!' And he carried the salad up to the girl.

The girl was dainty; she didn't put her fingers in the dish and pick out the lettuce leaves. No, she took a plate and a knife and fork, helped herself politely, and began to eat.

79

'It is truly delicious –' she began. But – *hee haw-aw-aw!* that was all she could say now; for she had swallowed a lettuce leaf, and she had turned into a pretty little donkey.

'Off with you, my pretty one!' said the hunter. And he gave her a slap, and she ran downstairs to join her companions in the courtyard.

The hunter washed the stain off his face and head and hands, so that the donkeys might recognize him. Then he, too, went out into the courtyard.

'Now you shall receive the reward of your faithlessness!' he said. And he tied the donkeys together with a rope and drove them away till he came to a mill. He tapped at the window: the miller put his head out, and asked him what he wanted.

'I have three tiresome animals here,' said the hunter. 'I don't want to keep them any longer. If you will take them off my hands, give them food and stabling, and do as I tell you with them, I will pay you well.'

'Well, why not?' said the miller. 'What do you want me to do with them?'

The hunter said, 'To the old donkey' (which was the witch) 'you are to give three beatings a day and only one meal. To this younger donkey' (which was the maid servant) 'you are to give one beating a day, and three meals. And to this pretty little darling' (which was the witch's daughter) 'you are to give no beating and three meals. For though she well deserves to be whipped, all the same my heart is tender to her.'

The hunter left the donkeys with the miller and went back to the castle. He found everything there that he wanted of food and drink, and a comfortable bed. He had taken his revenge, but all the same he was not particularly happy. He had no heart to whistle merrily as he used to do: emptiness was all about him, and loneliness, and he felt sad.

At the end of a week the miller came to the castle. He told the hunter that the old donkey – the one who had the three beatings and one meal every day – was now dead. 'The other two are still alive,' he said; 'they get their three meals a day, but they are so sad and downcast I don't think they can last much longer.'

Then the hunter took pity on them. He gave the miller the sum of money that had been agreed on, and bade him bring the donkeys back to the castle. When he saw the poor creatures, his heart smote him, they were so gaunt, they had such staring coats, and their heads hung down so dismally.

'Here, eat this, little donkeys,' he said. And he gave them each some leaves of the good lettuce, which he had kept carefully.

They ate the leaves, and immediately there they were, back in their human shapes. The witch's daughter fell at the hunter's feet and cried, 'Oh my love, my love, forgive me the wrong I have done you! My mother forced me to do it, and it was sorely against my will, for indeed I love you dearly. Your wishing cloak is hanging in the cupboard over there. And as for the bird's heart, I will drink a potion and give it back to you.'

But the hunter said, 'Keep the heart. What difference does it make? I cannot help but love you, and you shall be my wife.'

So they were married, and lived in the castle. She was a good, true wife, and he was a happy husband, who whistled merrily as he went hunting in the forest.

8 · Hansel and Gretel

Once upon a time there lived a little boy called Hansel, and a little girl called Gretel. Their mother was dead, but they had a step-mother, for their father, who was a woodcutter, had married again. They were very poor, and the stepmother did not love the children; she grudged them every crust they ate.

'If it were not for those two brats there would be more food for you and me,' she said to the children's father.

The man loved his children, but he was weak, and couldn't stand up to the stepmother's bullying. Yes, of course he ought to have kept her in her place, but he couldn't, and he didn't. And when the stepmother slapped and scolded the children, he just took his axe, went off to the wood, chopped away at the trees, and cried, 'Heaven help us!'

But since he wouldn't help himself, it seemed that Heaven wouldn't help him either. There came a famine in the land. Every-one was hungry, nobody could afford to buy wood, and the wood-cutter became poorer and poorer, until he had no money even to buy bread, and there was scarcely a crust left in the house.

One night the woodcutter lay in bed and moaned and groaned, 'Heaven help us! How are we going to feed the children to-morrow?'

'How are we going to feed *ourselves*, you mean!' said the step-mother. 'Plague take the children! Greedy little things – what use are they? Now you listen to me! Tomorrow morning we will take

83

Hansel and Gretel deep into the wood, light them a fire, give them each a crust, go to our work, and leave them. They will never find their way home, and we shall be rid of them once and for all.'

'Oh no! Oh no!' cried the woodcutter. 'We can't do that!'

'Fool!' said the stepmother. 'Do you want to see them die of hunger before our eyes? And die ourselves as well! Oh, all right, if that's your idea, go out and plane some planks to make our coffins!'

Well, she kept on at him and kept on at him, until he agreed to do as she said. Then she went to sleep and snored. But he lay awake moaning and thinking how wicked it was.

Hansel and Gretel were awake too; they were so hungry that they couldn't sleep. They heard what the stepmother planned to do, and Gretel began to cry. But Hansel said, 'Don't cry, little sister. It shan't happen!'

Then he got out of bed very quietly, put on his coat, crept downstairs and went out into the garden. The white pebbles on the garden path were gleaming in the moonlight. Hansel picked up the white pebbles till his pockets were bulging with them, and then he tiptoed quietly up to bed again.

'Try to sleep now, little sister,' he whispered to Gretel. 'All will be well.'

Before dawn, the stepmother came into the childrens' room, shouting, 'Get up, you two! You are coming into the forest with us to gather sticks.'

The children jumped up and dressed. The stepmother gave them each a crust of bread.

'Keep this for your dinners,' she said. 'If you eat it now, you won't get any more. Don't say I haven't warned you!'

Hansel's pockets were full of the white pebbles, so Gretel put the crusts in her apron, and they all started for the forest. They hadn't gone far when Hansel stopped and looked back at the house.

He did this again and again, and his father said, 'Hansel, what are you loitering for?'

'Oh Father,' said Hansel, 'I am looking at my white kitten, who is sitting on the roof and waving me good-bye.'

'You little fool!' said the stepmother. 'That isn't your white kitten! It's the sunrise lighting up the chimney.'

But Hansel hadn't really been looking at the kitten. He had been scattering white pebbles from his pocket along the way behind him.

Deeper and deeper they went into the forest. At last the stepmother stopped. They were in a gloomy place with big trees crowding all round them. 'Now,' she said to the children, 'gather sticks and light a fire.'

The children gathered sticks, and when the fire was burning, the stepmother said, 'See how kind we are! We are going to leave you to rest by this nice fire, whilst we go farther on to hew wood. When we have finished we'll come and fetch you.'

The stepmother and the woodcutter went away. The children sat by the fire and ate their crusts. 'Father can't be far away,' said Gretel. 'Listen! I can hear the blows of his axe!'

Hansel got up and walked round among the trees. When he came back, he said, 'That's not father's axe. Our stepmother has hung up a piece of wood on a rotten tree, and the wind is blowing it up and down, *slap, slap, slap!*'

Slap, slap, slap! That was the only sound they heard. The fire died down. Hansel put his arm round Gretel.

'Lay your head on my shoulder, little sister,' he said, 'and go to sleep.'

Gretel cuddled close to Hansel and went to sleep.

Slap, slap, slap! Hansel sat listening to the sound of the piece of wood hitting against the tree as the wind blew it up and down ... By and by he too fell asleep.

85

When the children woke up it was night. 'Oh Hansel, how dark it is!' said Gretel. 'What shall we do?'

'All will be well,' said Hansel. 'The moon will soon rise. Then we'll find our way home fast enough.'

'I'm frightened!' said Gretel.

'I'm not!' said Hansel. 'Look, here comes the moonlight!'

The moon shone among the forest trees, and there on the forest floor were the white pebbles that Hansel had dropped. They were shining like big silver coins. Hansel took his little sister's hand, and said, 'See, here is our way home!' And so they walked safely, guided by the glittering white pebbles, and at dawn reached their father's house and knocked at the door.

The stepmother opened it. She was so upset at seeing the children, whom she had thought never to see again, that she beat them and cried out, 'You wicked children! Wherever have you been? Why didn't you stay where we left you? We searched for you everywhere! We thought we'd lost you for good and all!'

But the father was delighted to have the children back. He had lain awake all night, thinking how wicked he had been.

That day he was able to sell a little wood and buy some food, and he cheered up and thought, 'Things are not so bad after all!' But in the days that followed he sold nothing.

A month later, when they went to bed, the stepmother gave him a poke in the ribs and said, 'Do you know that there is hardly anything left to eat – only half a loaf of bread! What is half a loaf between four of us? We must get rid of those children! We will take them deeper into the forest this time, so that they *can't* find their way back!'

'Oh no!' moaned the woodcutter.

'But I say *yes*!' cried the stepmother. 'You fool! Isn't it better that the children should die than that we all should perish?'

Hansel and Gretel were not asleep. They heard what the stepmother said. Again Hansel got up and crept downstairs. But the stepmother had locked the door and hidden the key. Now he couldn't get out to pick up the white pebbles, so he tiptoed up to bed again.

'Never mind, little sister,' he said to Gretel. 'In the morning I'll think of something.'

At dawn the stepmother came in and pushed the children out of bed. 'You are coming with us to the forest again,' she said. 'And see that you behave yourselves this time, and stay where we tell you!'

She gave each of the children a slice of bread and told them that would be all they would get for the day. Then the father, the stepmother and the two children set out for the forest.

And as they went, Hansel was loitering and looking behind him. His father said, 'Hansel, what are you loitering for?'

'I am looking at my little white dove,' said Hansel. 'She is sitting on the roof to coo me good-bye.'

'Fool!' said the stepmother. 'It is not your dove, but the morning sun shining on the white chimney.'

But Hansel was not really looking at his little dove. He was crumbling up his bread and dropping the crumbs along the way behind him.

Deep, deep, and deeper into the forest they went, much farther than they had ever been before. And in a dark little dell, with high trees and tangled thorn bushes growing all round it, the stepmother stopped.

'You may light a fire and wait here, children,' she said. 'Your father and I are going farther on to hew wood. When it is time for you to come home, we will fetch you.'

'And that will be never!' she said to herself, as she and the woodcutter walked away.

The children lit a fire; and when dinner-time came, Gretel broke her piece of bread in two and gave half to Hansel, because he had scattered all his as they came along. Then they fell asleep, and when they woke up it was night, and the moon was shining. Gretel jumped up and said, 'Take me home, Hansel!'

Hansel jumped up, and looked about him. What was this? The moonlight was shining on the ground, but there was no glittering white path of bread to guide them home – the birds had eaten every crumb.

'Never mind,' said Hansel, 'we shall soon find the way.'

But they didn't find the way. They walked all night and all the next day, and still the forest was round them. They were lost, quite lost, and they were hungry – oh, how hungry! They picked a few blackberries, and they found a few hazel nuts; and when night came again they made themselves a bed of leaves, and fell asleep, utterly worn out and very miserable.

In the morning they heard a bird singing. It was a white bird, and very beautiful. When it had finished its song, it spread its wings and flew off among the trees. 'Let us follow it!' said Hansel. 'Perhaps it is going to a place where there is something to eat.'

So they followed the bird, and by and by they came to a little house. The bird perched on the roof of the house and began to peck at it. It was the strangest little house that ever you saw: the walls were made of bread, and the roof was made of cake, and the windows were made of barley sugar.

'Oh, oh, oh!' Hansel was up on the roof, breaking off great lumps of cake, tossing some down to Gretel, and devouring some himself. The bird had flown away, but the children were munching, and munching, and munching.

Then a voice called from inside:

> '*Nibble, nibble, little mouse,*
> *Who's nibbling my house?*'

The children laughed and sang out:

> *''Tis heaven's own child,*
> *The wind so wild.'*

And they went on eating. They had pulled out a window pane now, and were busy sucking it, Hansel at one side and Gretel at the other, when the door opened, and a very old woman hobbled out, leaning on a stick.

The children dropped the barley sugar window-pane. They

thought they would run away, but the old woman was smiling and she didn't look angry. So Hansel said, 'Oh please, we didn't mean any harm. We are lost, and we were so very hungry!'

'Then come in, you poor little dears!' said the old woman. 'I'm very fond of children. You shall stay with me, and I'll give you something better to eat than cake and barley sugar!'

She took them each by the hand and led them in, and gave them a splendid meal of pancakes and milk and nuts and apples. And after that she showed them two little white beds, and said, 'Sleep now, you pretty dears, and forget all your sorrows.'

So Hansel and Gretel lay down in the two little beds, and felt they were in heaven. But the old woman was only pretending to be friendly. The children couldn't know it, but she was a wicked old witch, who had built her little cake and bread house on purpose to lure children into it. She *was* very fond of children, certainly – they were her favourite food. Once she had got them into her power, she fattened them up and cooked and ate them. And that was what she planned to do with Hansel and Gretel.

So she hobbled in to look at them while they slept, and chuckled, and said, 'The pretty little dears, I'll have them on toast! Oh ho! Ho ho! *Won't* they make a tasty dish!'

She seized Hansel up in her bony hands, carried him out to a little stable, and shut him in behind a grating. 'You may howl as loud as you like,' she said. 'There's no one to hear you but myself. And *I* don't mind!'

Then she went in to Gretel, shook her and screamed, 'Get up, you lazy girl. Go and draw water that I may cook your brother something good. I've put him in the stable for fattening. He's a bit on the skinny side at present; but I'll soon have him fat enough for eating!'

How poor Gretel sobbed and cried! But it was no use, she had to do what the witch told her. She had to fetch water, and stoke the fire, and help prepare the rich food that the witch cooked for Hansel. But Gretel herself got nothing but crab shells.

'Your turn for good food will come,' said the witch. 'But not until your brother's fit for table.'

Every morning the witch hobbled to the stable, stood in front of the grating, and called, 'Hansel, Hansel, put out your finger that I may feel if you are fat enough to eat yet.'

But Hansel didn't put out his finger; he put out a bone instead, and the witch, whose eyes were dim, pinched the bone and snuffed at it, and marvelled that Hansel didn't get fat.

A month went by, and still it seemed that Hansel didn't get any fatter. So then the witch lost patience and said, 'Fat or thin, into the oven you go!' She hobbled back to Gretel and said, 'Now, girl, get busy, light the fire and fill the kettle; first we'll bake the bread, and then we'll bake your brother.'

Oh how Gretel wept! 'If the wild beasts in the forest had but eaten us!' she sobbed. 'Then at least we should have died together!'

'Hold your noise!' said the witch. And she got so angry with Gretel's crying, that she made up her mind to cook and eat her as well, thin as she was. 'Now, girl,' she said, 'I've heated the oven, and kneaded the dough, come along to the bake house!'

She seized Gretel by the hair and dragged her out into the bake house. She opened the oven door, and said, 'Creep in and see if the oven is hot enough to put in the bread.'

Once Gretel was in the oven, you see, the witch meant to shut the door and roast her. But there came to Gretel an idea of how she might yet save Hansel, and she said, 'How can I get in? The oven's too small!'

'Too small! You stupid little goose!' said the witch. 'Why it's big enough for *me* to get in! Just you look!' And she stooped and put her head in at the oven door.

And Gretel gave her a push – and into the oven the old witch went, heels over head; and Gretel slammed the iron door and drew the bolt across it.

You may be sure Gretel didn't waste any time listening to the furious yells that came from the oven! She rushed to fetch the key of Hansel's cage, and unlocked the door, crying out, 'The witch is dead! The witch is dead! Oh Hansel, we are free!'

Hansel sprang out, and there they were, hugging one another and shouting and jumping for joy. Then, since there was nothing to stop them, they ran into the witch's house. There, in every corner of the room, they found chests full of precious stones – diamonds and pearls and rubies and emeralds.

'These stones are better than pebbles!' said Hans, as he crammed his pockets full of them. And Gretel said, 'I will take something home too!' And she filled her apron.

Meanwhile, in their home, their father was sorrowing. He had never known a moment's peace since he left the children in the forest. As the days passed, he reproached himself more and more bitterly. 'We did wrong,' he said to the stepmother. 'Oh, we did very wrong!'

She mocked him and scolded him, and argued with him and raged at him, but still he kept on saying, 'We did very wrong!' At last she could stand it no longer and decided to leave him and go back to her own people. But as she was going through the forest, the wolves came and gobbled her up, and that was the end of her.

The poor man was now all alone in his wretchedness. He could not know that his children were even then on their way back to him.

But they were. They were walking hand in hand through the forest, and by and by they came to a big lake. There was no bridge, there was no boat – how were they to get across?

Then they saw a duck swimming on the lake, and Gretel said, 'I'll ask the duck to help us!' And she sang out:

'Little duck, swim to land;
Two lost children, here we stand!
Little duck, for pity's sake,
Carry us across the lake!'

The duck swam to shore; Hansel got on the duck's back, and told Gretel to get up beside him. But Gretel said, 'No, no! We shall be too heavy for the poor bird! She shall take us one at a time.'

So the good little bird ferried Hansel over, and then came back for Gretel, and carried her across also. When they were on the other side of the lake – goodness me! They found themselves in a piece of the forest that they knew quite well: and there was their father's house in the distance.

They ran, they reached the house, they pushed the door open, calling out, 'Father! Father!'

He was sitting by the empty hearth, with the tears running down his cheeks, too miserable even to get up and light the fire. But when he saw the children, he leaped up, and shouted for joy. They told him all their adventures, and flung down at his feet all the treasure they had brought home. 'We are rich!' they told him. 'We need never go hungry again!'

And they never did go hungry again, but lived happily – oh so happily! – ever after.

9 · Tatterhood

Once upon a time there lived a king and queen who had no children. The queen mourned all day, and nothing would make her happy. One day she went out to walk in the forest and came to a little house. And she sat down outside the little house and wept.

And a little old woman came out of the house, and said, 'Why do you weep?'

'I weep because I have no children,' said the queen.

Now this little old woman was a witch, but she was a good and kind one; for such witches do exist in the world, although their number is but few. So this good little witch said to the queen, 'I can promise you a child if you will do as I say.'

'I will do anything!' said the queen.

'Go home,' said the good little witch, 'and at bedtime take two pails of water, and wash in each of them. When you have washed, throw the water from both pails under the bed. Look under the bed next morning, and you will see that two flowers have sprung up, one fair and one ugly. The fair one you must eat; the ugly one you must not touch. Remember especially not to touch the ugly one. And may all go well with you!'

The good little witch went back into her house, and the queen went home. That night she had two pails of water brought into her bedroom, and washed herself in both of them. When she had washed, she emptied the water from both the pails under the bed, and lay down and slept in hope. And in the morning, when she

94

looked under the bed, lo! there were the two flowers. One flower was ugly, with black petals, and a pinched and starved look about it. The other flower was silvery white and softly shining, most beautiful, like a risen star. The queen took up the beautiful flower and ate it. Its perfumed flavour was very sweet – so sweet that the queen longed for more. And before she thought what she was doing, she had eaten the ugly flower as well. And it had no taste at all about it.

Well, well, sure enough, in a few months after that, the queen gave birth to a baby girl. The baby had a mat of ragged black hair and an ashen grey face. It was very ugly. And as soon as ever that baby was born, it bawled out, 'Mamma!'

'If I'm your mamma,' said the queen, 'God give me grace to mend my ways!'

'Oh, never worry yourself about *me*,' said the hideous little baby. 'The one who comes after me will be better looking.'

Somehow or other this hideous little baby got hold of a wooden spoon and a goat. And before she was a week old, she was riding about on that goat and banging with the wooden spoon. The queen couldn't bear the sight of her, and was as unhappy as she had been before – until she had another baby girl. This second baby was as beautiful as a new risen star. Her eyes were as darkly blue as the night sky, and her hair shone like silver.

The queen called this second baby Berenice, which is the name of a star, and she loved her beyond all telling. But the elder sister they called Tatterhood, because she would go about in a ragged hood to cover up her lank locks of black hair. The queen did not love Tatterhood any better as the years passed. And the royal nurses tried to shut her up in a room by herself. But it was no good. Wherever Berenice went, there Tatterhood would be also. And though the queen could not understand it, Berenice loved her ugly sister dearly.

95

Well, one Christmas eve, when the sisters were nearly grown up, Tatterhood was riding about the palace on her goat, and banging away with her wooden spoon – pretending, no doubt, that she was a knight in armour – when she heard a screaming and a clattering in the gallery outside the queen's bedroom. She galloped off to the queen and said, 'What is all the racket going on up there?'

'Whatever it is,' said the queen, 'it has nothing to do with *you*. Go away, and keep quiet, if you can!'

But Tatterhood wouldn't go away and keep quiet. She said that whatever it was, she was going up there to fight it. So then the queen told her that it was a pack of witches who had come there to keep Christmas. 'They come and they go,' she said. 'We can do nothing about it.'

'Oh can't we?' said Tatterhood.

'Go away,' said the queen.

'Yes, I am going,' said Tatterhood. 'I am going up to the gallery to drive the witches out. But you must keep all the doors that lead into the gallery shut and locked while I am about it.'

'*Go away!*' said the queen again.

Tatterhood went away. She went up to the gallery, and the gallery was swarming with witches. They leaped upon Tatterhood in a fury, but she banged about her with her wooden spoon, and swept them along like autumn leaves before her. The whole palace creaked and groaned as if every joint and beam was being torn out of its place: but the witches fled before Tatterhood's wooden spoon. Of the whole pack of them there was but one witch left, when one of the doors of the gallery opened softly (for the silly queen had not heeded what Tatterhood said about locking them) and Berenice peeped in.

'What is happening . . .' began Berenice. But that last witch had seen the shining head, and before Tatterhood could stop her, that witch had snatched the shining head from Berenice's shoulders and

put a calf's head in its place. Now poor little Berenice could say nothing but 'Moo'.

The queen was in hysterics, the king was raving, but Tatterhood rounded on them with fierce words for not locking the gallery doors, and they fell silent. 'Give me a ship in full trim,' said Tatterhood. 'I will set my sister free if I can. I want no captain, I want no sailors. My sister and I must set out on this voyage alone.'

There was no denying her; that ship she must have, and she got it. Tatterhood took her goat and her wooden spoon, and went aboard. Her poor little calf-headed sister followed her. Away they sailed, and Tatterhood steered her ship to the land where the witches lived.

When she came to the landing place, she told Berenice to stay on board, but she herself got astride her goat, took her wooden spoon and rode up to the witches' castle. When she got there, one of the windows was open, and she saw Berenice's lovely head hung up on the window frame. In through the window she leaped on her goat, snatched the head, and leaped out again.

Now the witches were after her, thick as a swarm of angry buzzing hornets, but she banged about her with her wooden spoon, and the goat leaped and snorted and butted with its horns; and so fierce were they, the pair of them, that the witches fell back. Tatterhood reached the ship, took the calf's head off her sister, put Berenice's own lovely head back in its place again, and flung the calf's head after the retreating witches.

'Now my lovely one,' she said to Berenice, 'I am going to take you on a long, long voyage.'

'I will go anywhere you like, dear sister,' said Berenice.

They sailed on and on and on. They sailed for a year, and for two years, and for three years. In the third year they came to the shores of a new country, and Tatterhood drove her ship into harbour.

Now the palace of the king of that country was near the harbour;

and this king was a widower with an only son. The king looked out
of a window and saw the strange ship; and he sent messengers to
the harbour to find out where the ship came from and who owned
it. But when the king's men came to the ship, they saw not a soul
on board but Tatterhood. There she was, waving her wooden spoon
and riding her goat round and round the deck at top speed. Her
hood had fallen from her head, her lank black hair was streaming
out behind her, and her queer ugly face was all agrin like a goblin's.
It was the strangest sight the men had ever seen.

'Halloo, halloo!' they shouted. 'Is there no one but you aboard?
Where is the captain, where are the sailors?'

'Before you, before you!' cried Tatterhood, as she galloped
round.

'Is there no one but you aboard?' they shouted.

'There is also my sister.'

'Then let us see your sister,' shouted the king's men.

'No one shall see her, unless the king comes himself,' cried
Tatterhood. And she galloped her goat till the deck thundered.

The men went back to the palace and told the king of the strange
sight they had seen. The king was for seeing this strange sight for
himself, and he hurried down to the harbour. As soon as she saw
him, Tatterhood called to him to come aboard. And as soon as he
had come aboard, she got off her goat and went down to the cabin
to fetch Berenice.

Never in his life had the king imagined that a maiden could be so
beautiful. He fell in love with Berenice on the spot. He took both
the sisters back to the palace with him and made much of them.
Now nothing would satisfy him but that he must have Berenice for
his wife.

But Tatterhood said, 'Certainly not! You shall not have my
sister unless your son will have me.'

The king sent for the prince. Oh dear! The prince gave one look at Tatterhood, and covered his eyes. 'No, no, I will not have her! Nothing shall induce me to marry that fright!'

'As you please,' said Tatterhood. And she took Berenice back to the ship. 'In a week we set sail, and you will never see us again,' she said to the king.

The king was in despair. He threatened to disinherit his son. The prince sulked, the king raged, the whole court was in a turmoil. The days passed; the week was nearly up; and there was Tatterhood galloping her goat round and round the deck of the ship – but there was no sign of Berenice. The king went down to the harbour. 'Let me but look upon her once again!' he cried to Tatterhood.

But Tatterhood shouted, 'You know my terms' – and went on madly galloping her goat.

The king went back to the palace and said to the prince, 'If you do not yield by tomorrow, I will cut off your head!'

The prince stuck out his jaw and said, 'I will not marry that fright.'

The king's counsellors came to the prince; the courtiers came to the prince; the lords-in-waiting and the ladies-in-waiting came to the prince. They knelt before him, they entreated him. 'Do not throw your precious life away,' they implored him; 'marry her, and when she is your wife you can shut her up in a palace by herself.'

'Very well,' said the prince at last. 'I will marry her, and when she is my wife I will shut her up in a dungeon. For what can she be but a witch?'

Now the king was all smiles. He would have embraced his obedient son; but the prince pushed him away. The king didn't heed; he hurried to the harbour and bade Tatterhood bring Berenice to the palace. He hastened on the preparations for the wedding. There was such a baking and a brewing, such a running about of tailors and dressmakers, such a dressing up of lords and ladies, such a preening before mirrors, such a trying on of jewels and coronets, such an arriving of musicians and singers, such a gilding of chariots and grooming of horses as the realm had never seen before. But the prince would have no new clothes. And as for Tatterhood – there she was, prepared to go to church riding on her goat and waving her wooden spoon.

And that's the way Tatterhood did go to church.

First the king drove off with his bride in a golden coach drawn by ten prancing white horses. And the bride was so lovely that the people crowded the streets to see her pass and gazed after her till she was out of sight. Then came the coaches with the counsellors, and the lords and the ladies – a very grand procession. And last of all came the prince on horseback with his head down; and beside him rode Tatterhood on her goat, waving her wooden spoon.

'Why don't you say something?' said Tatterhood to the prince.

And the prince answered gloomily, 'What is there for me to say?'

'Well, you might at least ask me why I ride upon this ugly goat,' said Tatterhood.

'Why do you ride upon that ugly goat?' said the prince.

'Is it an ugly goat?' said Tatterhood. 'Oh no! It's the grandest horse that ever a bride rode on.'

And lo, the goat became a horse; and that horse was the most magnificent animal that ever trod the earth.

'I knew she was a witch!' thought the doleful prince. But he said no word; and they rode on in silence, until Tatterhood said again, 'Why don't you say something?'

And again the prince answered gloomily, 'What is there for me to say?'

'You might at least ask me why I ride with this ugly spoon in my fist.'

'All right. Why do you ride with that ugly spoon in your fist?' said the doleful prince.

'Is it an ugly spoon? Why, it's the loveliest silver wand that ever a bride carried,' said Tatterhood.

And lo, the wooden spoon became a silver wand, shining so brightly in the sunlight that the prince's eyes were dazzled.

But he said no word. And they rode on in silence, until Tatterhood said again,

'Why don't you say something?'

And the doleful prince answered, 'What is there for me to say?'

'You might at least ask why I wear this ragged hood on my head.'

'Well then, why do you wear that ragged hood?'

'Is it a ragged hood?' said she. 'Why, it's the brightest golden crown that ever a bride wore.'

And lo! on the instant, the tattered hood became a golden crown.

They rode on in silence: until Tatterhood said,

'Why don't you say something?'

'I have nothing to say,' answered the doleful prince.

'You might at least ask me why my face is so ugly and ashen-grey.'

'All right,' said the prince peevishly. 'Why is your face so ugly and ashen-grey?'

'Am I ugly?' said Tatterhood. 'Why, you think my sister beautiful; but I am more beautiful than she is.'

And lo! when the prince looked at her, there she was – a maiden more lovely than all the stars in heaven.

'Oh, my beautiful one!' gasped the prince. 'Who and what are you?'

'As you see me, so I am,' said Tatterhood. And she laughed.

You may be sure the prince didn't hang his head or wish to tarry after that. The pair of them rode on at a brisk pace, and soon caught up with the bridal procession. Now the people who crowded the streets were not looking at Berenice any longer: they had eyes for no one but the beautiful Tatterhood. They cheered and cheered as she and the prince rode by.

So they all arrived at the church and were married: the king and Berenice, the prince and Tatterhood. And Berenice said, 'Now you see my sister as she really is. She was always beautiful to me.'

They rejoiced together; they held the bridal feast, and all went merrily.

10 · The White Dove

A long time ago, in a country by the sea, there lived a king and queen who had two sons. And those two sons were reckless lads. One stormy day they put to sea in a little boat to go fishing. The wind howled, and they laughed. The waves dashed over the boat, and still they laughed. But when they were a long way from land, the wind tore their sail to ribbons, and the waves washed their oars overboard; and there they were, tossing about with the waves drenching them, while they clung to their seats to keep from being pitched out of the boat.

'Brother,' said one prince, 'shall we ever reach home again?'

'No, brother,' said the other. 'It seems we shall not.'

Then they looked through the spray and saw the strangest vessel in the world come speeding towards them over the rolling billows. It was a kneading-trough, and in it sat an old witch, beating the waves with two long wooden ladles.

'Hey, my lads!' she yelled. 'What will you give me to send you safely home?'

'Anything we have!' shouted the princes.

'Then give me your brother,' yelled the witch.

'We have no brother,' shouted the princes.

'Aye, but you will have,' yelled the witch.

'Even so,' shouted the eldest prince, 'should our mother bear another son, he will not belong to us.'

'So we can't give him away!' shouted the other prince.

'Then you can rot in the salt sea, both of you!' yelled the witch. 'But I think your mother would rather keep the two sons she has than the one she hasn't yet got.' And she rowed off in her kneading-trough.

If the storm had been fierce before, it was now furious. The princes' little boat was flung up high on the waves one moment,

and the next sucked deep down, with the waves towering over it. It pitched and rolled and wallowed and filled with water.

'Brother,' said one prince, 'we are going to drown.'

'Ah, how our mother will grieve!' said the other prince.

105

'Brother,' said the first prince, 'the old witch was right. Our mother would rather keep *us* than a son she may never have.'

So they shouted after the witch, and she turned her trough and came rowing back to them.

'Have you changed your minds?' she yelled.

'Yes,' shouted the princes. 'If you will save us from drowning, we promise you the brother we may never have.'

Immediately the wind ceased howling and the sea grew flat. A current caught the boat and drove it swiftly over the calm water. The current brought the boat ashore just under the king's castle. The princes sprang out, and ran into the castle. The queen, who had been watching the storm from a window, flung her arms round them.

'Oh my sons!' cried the queen. 'If you had been drowned I could not have lived!'

And one prince whispered to the other, 'We did right to promise.'

But they said nothing to their mother about what they had promised, either then, or a year later, when a brother was born to them. The new little prince was a beautiful child; and because he was so much younger than his brothers, the queen did her best to spoil him. But it seemed he was unspoilable. He loved his brothers, and they loved him: and still they said nothing about their promise to give him to the witch. For some time, indeed, they lived in dread lest the witch should come and claim him; but, as the years passed, and the little prince grew up, and still the witch did not come, the two elder princes almost succeeded in forgetting the promise they had made.

Now the youngest prince was studious; and often, long after the rest of the household had gone to their beds, he would sit in a little room downstairs, reading and thinking. One night, as he so sat, the wind began to howl and the sea to roar, the stars disappeared behind mountainous black clouds, and the rain came down in torrents. The prince lifted his head, listened for a moment, and went on reading. Then came three loud knocks on the door; and before the prince could open it, in darted the witch, with her kneading-trough on her back.

'Come with me!' she said.

The prince said, 'Why should I go with you?'

'Because you belong to me,' said the witch. And she told him all about that day on which his brothers came near to drowning, and how she had saved their lives, and what they had promised.

The young prince closed his book and stood up. 'Since you saved my brothers' lives and they gave you their promise, I am ready to go with you,' he said.

He followed the witch out of the castle and down to the sea. The witch launched her kneading-trough. They both got into it, and away they went, pitching and tossing over the raging waves, till they came to the witch's home.

'Now you are my servant,' said the witch, 'and everything I tell you to do, you must do. If you cannot do what I tell you to do, you are of no use to me. And when things are of no use to me, I throw them into the sea.'

'I will do my best,' said the young prince.

The witch then took him to a barn which was piled high with feathers of different colours and sizes. 'Arrange these feathers in their heaps,' she said, 'and let the feathers in each heap be of the same colour and the same size. I am going out now, and when I come back in the evening I shall expect the task to be finished.'

'I will do my best,' said the prince again.

'Ho, ho! But will your best be good enough?' said she.

'That I cannot tell,' said he.

The witch went away then, and the prince began his task. He worked very hard all day, and towards evening he had all the feathers except one goose quill arranged in their heaps – size to size and colour to colour. He was just going to place the goose quill on top of a heap of big white feathers, when there came a whirlwind that blew the feathers all about the barn. And when the whirlwind had passed and the feathers had settled, they were in worse confusion than they had been at first.

The prince set to work again; but there was now only an hour left before the time the witch would return. 'I cannot possibly finish by then!' he said aloud. But still he went on with his task.

Then he heard a tapping at the window, and a little voice said:

> 'Coo, coo, coo, please let me in,
> If we work together, we'll always win.'

It was a white dove, who was perched outside the glass, and was tapping on it with her beak.

The prince opened the window, and the dove flew in. She set to work with her beak, he set to work with his hands; he worked swiftly, but she worked a hundred times more swiftly. By the time the hour was passed, all the feathers were neatly arranged in their heaps. The dove flew out of the window, and the witch came in at the door.

'So,' said she, 'I see princes have neat fingers!'

'I have done my best,' said the prince.

'And tomorrow you must do better,' said she. And she gave him some supper and sent him to bed.

In the morning she took him outside and showed him a great pile of firewood. 'Split this into small pieces for me,' she said. 'That is easy work, and will soon be done. But you must have it all ready by the time I come home.'

'I will do my best,' said the young prince.

'If your best is not good enough, the sea is waiting,' said the witch. And off she went.

The prince set to work with a will; he chipped and chopped till the sweat ran off him. But the more wood he chopped up, the more there seemed to be left unchopped. Yes, there was no doubt of it – the pile of unchopped firewood was growing and growing. He flung down his axe in despair. What could he do?

Then the white dove came flying, settled on the pile of wood, and said:

> '*Coo, coo, coo, take the axe by the head,*
> *And chop with the handle end instead.*'

The prince took the axe by the head and began chopping with the handle; and the firewood flew into small pieces of its own accord. The prince chopped, the dove took the little pieces in her beak and arranged them in a tidy pile. In no time at all, it seemed, the task was finished.

Then the dove flew up on to the prince's shoulder. And he stroked its soft feathers. 'How can I ever thank you?' he said. And he kissed its little red beak.

Immediately the dove vanished; and there, at the prince's side, stood a beautiful maiden.

'How can I ever thank *you*,' said the maiden, 'for the kiss that has disenchanted me?'

She told him that she was a princess, whom the witch had stolen and turned into a white dove.

'But the power of a grateful kiss is stronger than all the witch's enchantments,' said the maiden. 'And perhaps together we may find a way to escape her. That is, if you like me well enough?'

'I love you!' said the prince. And truly, so he did.

'Then listen carefully to what I am going to tell you,' said the princess. 'When the witch comes home ask her to grant you a wish, as a reward for having accomplished the tasks she has set you. If she agrees, ask her to give you the princess who is flying about in the shape of a white dove. She will not want to do so; she will try to deceive you; but take this red silk thread and tie it round my little finger. Then you will recognize me, whatever shape she may turn me into.'

So the prince tied the red silk thread round the princess's little finger, and she turned into a dove again, and flew away. The prince sat down by the pile of split firewood to wait until the witch came home. And very soon he saw her coming, with her kneading-trough on her back.

'Well, well, well!' said she. 'I see you are a clever fellow! I think I shall be pleased with you yet!'

'If you are pleased with me,' said the prince, 'perhaps you will be willing to grant me a little pleasure also, and give me something I have taken a fancy to?'

'Well, well, that's only reasonable,' said the witch, who was in a very good temper. 'Tell me what it is you wish for, and if it is any little thing that is in my power to give you, I promise I will do so.'

'There is a princess here, who flies about in the shape of a white dove,' said the prince. 'It is that princess I want.'

The witch screeched with laughter. 'What nonsense are you talking? As if princesses ever flew around in the shape of white doves!'

'Nevertheless, I ask for that princess,' said the prince.

'Well, well, if you *will* have a princess,' said the witch, 'you must take the only sort I have.' And she went away round the back of the house, and came again dragging by one long ear a shaggy little grey ass. 'Will you have this?' she said. 'You can't get any other kind of princess here.'

The prince looked at the little ass, and saw a thin thread of red silk round one of its hoofs. 'Yes, I will have it,' he said.

'It is too small for you to ride, and too old to draw a cart,' said the witch. 'Why should you have it? It is no use to you at all!' And she dragged the little ass away, and came back with a tottering, trembling old hag of a woman who was blind in one eye, and hadn't a tooth in her head.

'Here's a pretty princess for you!' said the witch. 'What do you say, will you have her? She was born a princess, and she's the only one I've got.'

'Yes, I will have her,' said the prince, for he saw that the old hag had a thin thread of red silk bound about her little finger.

He took the old hag by the hand. Behold – there stood the princess! The witch flew into such a terrible rage that she danced about and screamed and smashed everything within her reach, so that the splinters flew about the heads of the prince and princess. But she had promised the prince that he should have his wish, and she had to keep her word. She said to herself, 'Yes, they shall be married. But when they *are* married, oh ho! let them look out!'

So the day of the wedding was fixed, and the princess said to the prince, 'At the wedding feast you may eat what you please, but you must not drink anything at all; for the witch will put a spell on both the water and the wine, and if you drink you will forget me.'

'How could I ever forget you?' said the prince.

'Nevertheless, do not drink,' said the princess.

A whole troop of witches came to the wedding feast. It was a hideous affair, and all the food was so highly seasoned that the prince's throat was dry and burning. At last he could bear his thirst no longer, and he stretched out his hand for a cup of wine. But the princess was keeping watch over him; she gave the prince's arm a push with her elbow: all the wine was spilled over the table-cloth, and the cup rolled off the table and fell on the floor.

When the witch saw that she had been again foiled by the princess, she flew once more into a terrible rage. She leaped up and laid about her among the plates and dishes, till the splinters flew about the room. The other witches howled with laughter, and joined in the fun, smashing everything they could lay hands on. But when the clamour was at its height, the princess took the prince by the hand, and whispered, 'Come!'

They ran up to the bridal chamber which had been got ready for them. And the princess said, 'The witch had to keep her promise, and we are married. But it was sore against her will, and now she will seek to destroy us. We must escape while we may.'

From having lived so long with the witch, the princess had learned some magic. Now she took two pieces of wood, spoke some whispered words to them, and laid them side by side in the bed.

'These will answer for us if the witch calls,' she said. 'Now take the flower pot from the ledge, and the bottle of water from the table, and help me down out of the window.'

The prince picked up the flower pot and the water bottle, helped the princess down out of the window, and scrambled out after her.

Then off they ran, hand in hand, through the dark night.

The nearest way to reach the prince's home was across the sea. But they had no boat, so they had to run round the shore of a great bay. All night they were running. Meanwhile, at midnight, the witch went to the door of the bridal chamber, and called, 'Are you sleeping yet?'

And the two pieces of wood answered from the bed, 'No, we are waking.'

The witch went away. Before dawn she came again to the door of the bridal chamber, and called, 'Are you sleeping yet?'

And the two pieces of wood answered from the bed, 'We are waking still. But leave us now to sleep.'

The witch chuckled, 'Sleep soundly,' she muttered. 'You will not wake again in a hurry! For dawn brings a new day. Your wedding night will then be over. And what did I promise you? No more than that!'

She went to her window and watched impatiently for the rising of the new day. As soon as the rim of the sun appeared above the sea, she rushed to the bridal chamber again. But this time she did not stand at the door. She flung the door open, and bounded into the room.

'I have you now!' she screamed.

But what did she see? No prince, no princess: only two blocks of wood lying side by side in the bed.

'Ah, ah, ah!' she shrieked. She seized upon the blocks of wood and flung them to the floor so violently that they flew into hundreds of pieces. Then she rushed off after the runaways.

The prince and princess had run on through the night. They were still running now along the shore of the bay, with the first beams of the sun on their faces.

Said the princess, 'Look round. Do you see anything behind us?'

Said the prince, 'Yes, I see a dark cloud, far away.'

Said the princess, 'Throw the flower pot over your head.'

The prince threw the flower pot over his head, and a huge range of hills rose up behind them. The witch came to the hills; she tried to climb them. But they were smooth and slippery as glass; every time she clambered up a little way, she slid down again. There was nothing for it but to run round the whole range, and that took her a very long time.

The prince and princess were still running along the shore of the bay. By and by the princess said again, 'Look round. Do you see anything behind us?'

'Yes,' said the prince, 'the big black cloud is there again.'

Said the princess, 'Throw the bottle of water over your head.'

The prince threw the bottle of water over his head, and a huge, turbulent lake spread out behind them. The witch came to the lake. It was so huge and so rough that she had to go all the way home again to fetch her kneading-trough before she could cross it.

By the time the witch had crossed the lake and was pelting on again, the prince and princess had rounded the bay and reached the castle which was the prince's home. They climbed over the wall of the keep, and were just about to clamber into the castle through an open window, when the witch caught up with them.

'Ah! Ah! Ah! I have you now!' she screamed.

But the princess turned and blew upon the witch. A great flock of white doves flew out of the princess's mouth. They fluttered and flapped about the witch; she was completely hidden by their beating wings. And when the doves rose into the air and flew away, there was no witch. There was only a great grey stone standing outside the window.

The prince led his princess into his father's castle. 'I have come back to you,' he said to the king and queen. 'And I have brought my bride with me.'

How they all rejoiced! The prince's two elder brothers came and knelt at his feet and begged his forgiveness. 'You shall inherit the kingdom,' they said, 'and we will be forever your faithful subjects.' And, in the course of time, when the old king died, that was what happened.

In the meantime, and ever afterwards, they lived in happiness.

11 · *Johnny and the Witch-Maidens*

There was once an orphan lad called Johnny, and he set out to look for work. He walked and he walked, a long, long way, but he couldn't find anyone to employ him. At last, close by a forest, he saw a little house, and on the doorstep of the little house sat an old man. This old man looked sad, as well he might, for he had no eyes in his head, either seeing or blind – but just empty spaces where his eyes should be.

Behind the little house was a shed; and from the shed came the bleating of many goats.

'Ah, my poor goats, my poor goats!' sighed the old man. 'You should go to pasture, and how willingly I would take you! But, poor goats, I cannot take you, because I am blind. And I have no one to send with you.'

So then Johnny spoke up, and said, 'Daddy, send me!'

'Who speaks?' said the old man

And Johnny answered, 'An orphan lad. One who seeks work, and will surely do his best. If you take me for your servant, I will pasture your goats, and I will look after you, also.'

The old man said, 'Step up close that I may feel you.'

Johnny stepped up close. The old man passed his hand over Johnny's face, and said, 'I think you are a good, honest lad. Yes, I will take you for my servant. Go into the house and get yourself a bite to eat. Don't spare of what there is, for you must be hungry.'

Johnny *was* hungry. He went in, found milk and bread, and cheese and apples, and ate and drank his fill. Then he came out again, and said:

'Daddy, what about you? Shall I bring you food?'

'No, no,' said the old man. 'I am seldom hungry. I have no heart to eat since my eyes were stolen from me. If *your* hunger is satisfied, will you now drive my goats to pasture, for the crying of the poor creatures troubles me sorely. Aye, drive them to the best pasture you can find; but don't lead them to yonder hill above the forest. If you do, witch-maidens will come to you and put you to sleep; and when you are asleep they will steal your eyes from you, as they have stolen mine from me.'

Johnny laughed. 'Never fear, Daddy! No witch-maidens shall steal *my* eyes!'

The old man sighed and said, 'Dear lad, have a care!'

And Johnny laughed again. 'Surely I will have a care, Daddy!'

So Johnny drove the goats to pasture on some waste land below the forest, and brought them back in the evening full and contented. He milked the nanny-goats and made cheese and butter; he also found some flour, and heated the oven, and baked bread. He was busy the day long and the evening long, and the old man praised him and said, 'You are a lad in a million! We should soon have been underground, my poor goats and I, if the good God had not sent you.'

Johnny laughed. 'If you are satisfied, Daddy, so am I.'

And then, one day, Johnny looked up at the hill above the forest, and said to himself, 'Up there are rocks where the goats may climb and leap, and the turf among the rocks is green and sweet, and there are young trees on the hill whose tender shoots they will delight to nibble. Why should I shepherd the poor creatures on the flat wastes where there is nothing to amuse

116

them? I will take them up on to the hill. *I* am not afraid of witch-maidens!'

So what did he do but cut three prickly shoots of bramble and put them in his hat: and then he led the goats up on to the hill.

A fine time the goats had of it up there, leaping and climbing, and nibbling the sweet turf and the tree shoots, and the little kids playing 'king of the castle' – perching themselves on the top of the rocks, and butting each other off.

And Johnny sat down in the shade of a rock, and laughed to watch them.

He hadn't sat there long when he heard a voice saying, 'God bless you, young goat herd!' And there at his side stood a most beautiful damsel. She was dressed in white, her hair was long and shining and black as night, her eyes were black as sloes, her lips were red as cherries, her skin was lily-fair, and she was carrying a basket of apples.

She showed him the basket and said, 'See what beautiful apples grow in my garden! I'll give you one, that you may taste how good they are.' And she took a rosy apple from the basket and held it out to him.

'Oh ho!' thought Johnny, 'here we have witch-maiden number one! If I eat that apple I shall fall asleep, and then, no doubt, she will tear out my eyes and leave me with empty sockets, like my poor old master.'

So he said, 'Thank you all the same; but my master has an apple tree in his garden. His apples are much finer than yours, and I have eaten my fill of them. I couldn't eat another morsel.'

'Oh well,' said the damsel, 'it's not I that am compelling you!'
And she walked away.

Soon afterwards there came another, even more beautiful, damsel. She had a red rose in her hand, and she held it out to Johnny. 'God bless you, young goat herd! See what a beautiful rose I have just picked in my garden! Its smell is sweeter than honey – just you smell it and see!'

'Oh ho!' thought Johnny. 'Here we have witch-maiden number two. If I smell that rose I shall fall asleep; then she will pluck out my eyes, and I shall be sightless like my poor old master!'

So he said, 'Thank you all the same. But my master has a garden where roses grow that are much finer than yours. I have smelled my fill of them.'

The damsel scowled and looked quite wicked and ugly. 'Oh well, if you won't – let it alone!' she said.

And she walked away.

Very soon there came yet another damsel; and if the first and second had been beautiful, she was much more so.

'God bless you, young goat herd!'

'Thank you, pretty one.'

'Indeed you are a handsome lad!' said the damsel. 'But you would be more handsome if your hair was not so untidy. Come, let me comb it for you!'

'Oh ho!' thought Johnny, 'here we have witch-maiden number three! If she passes her comb through my hair she will put me to sleep. And then she will tear out my eyes, as she did my poor old master's.'

But he said nothing. He sat still where he was, and smiled at the damsel. Then, just as she came close up to him to comb his hair, he took off his hat, drew out a bramble shoot, and *slap, slap*, struck her with it on both her hands.

'Help! Help!' screamed the damsel, but she could not move from the place. She began to weep; but Johnny cared nothing for her tears. He bound her hands together with the bramble.

Then up ran the other two damsels, and begged Johnny to unbind their sister and let her go.

'Unbind her yourselves,' said Johnny.

118

'We cannot,' they cried, 'we have such tender hands, the thorns would tear us!'

'In that case, she must stay bound,' said Johnny.

So then the two damsels came up close and began trying to loose their sister from the bramble. But Johnny took the two other bramble shoots from his hat, and *slap, slap!* he struck the other two damsels' hands with the shoots. They shrieked and cried, but they could not move, and he bound their hands together.

'See, now I've got you, you wicked witch-maidens!' said he. 'Why did you tear out my master's eyes?'

And he left them all three standing by the rock, weeping and lamenting, and drove the goats home to the old man.

'Come, Daddy,' said he. 'I've found someone who'll give you your eyes again.'

And he led the old man to the rock on the hill.

'Now,' said he to the first witch-maiden. 'Tell me where my master's eyes are, or I'll throw you into yonder river and drown you!'

'I don't know where they are,' said the witch-maiden.

'All right,' said Johnny, 'come and be drowned!' And he lifted her up, and made as if to carry her down to the river that flowed at the bottom of the hill, when she screamed out, 'Don't drown me, Johnny, don't drown me! I'll give you the old man's eyes!'

She led him to a cavern by the river, and in the cavern was a great heap of eyes of all sizes, large and small, and of all colours: blue, green, brown, black and red. She turned over this heap of eyes, and took out two.

'Here, these are his eyes!' she said.

And Johnny fitted the eyes into the old man's head.

But the old man began to cry, and said, 'Alas! Alas! These are not my eyes! I see nothing but owls!'

Johnny was in a rage then; he seized up the witch-maiden and threw her into the river. And the river carried her away.

He went back to the rock and said to the second witch-maiden, 'Give me my master's eyes.'

'I don't know where they are,' said the second witch-maiden.

'All right,' said Johnny. 'Come and be drowned!' He lifted her up, and made as if to carry her down to the river, when she screamed out, 'Don't, Johnny! Don't! I'll give you the old man's eyes!'

They went down to the cavern, and she turned over the heap of eyes, and picked out two. Johnny fitted them into the old man's head, and said, 'Can you see now, Daddy?'

But the old man cried, 'Alas! Alas! These are not my eyes! I see nothing but wolves!'

So then Johnny seized up the second witch-maiden and threw her into the river. And the river carried her away.

Johnny went back to the rock and said to the third witch-maiden, 'I've stood no nonsense with your first sister, I've stood no nonsense with your second sister, and I'll stand no nonsense with you. Come, give me my master's eyes.'

'I will give them to you,' she said.

They went down again to the cavern, and she picked two eyes out of the heap.

'Are these the right ones?' said Johnny.

'They are,' said she.

'They had better be,' said Johnny, 'or it will be the worse for you! Come, Daddy, let's fit them in!'

'Oh dear! Oh dear!' wailed the old man when the eyes were put in his head. 'Now I see nothing but pike!'

'You she-devil!' cried Johnny. And he picked her up and carried her to the river. 'Now, one, two, three!' And he swung her out over the water.

But she clung to him and screamed, 'Don't, don't, Johnny! I will give you the old man's proper eyes!'

Johnny didn't throw her into the river. Perhaps he had never meant to, because, if he did throw her in, how was he to get back his master's eyes? So he carried her back to the cave, and she grovelled and scrabbled among the heap, and from the very bottom of it brought up two bright blue eyes.

Johnny put them into his master's head, and the old man cried, 'Praise be, these *are* my eyes! I can see everything clearly again. I can see the sky, I can see the earth, I can see you – but I can't see that wicked witch-maiden, where is she?'

Johnny looked round – the witch-maiden had vanished. Nor did she or her sisters ever come back to trouble them again.

So Johnny and his master went home together. Johnny laughed, and the old man laughed. Johnny looked after the goats, and the old man made the cheeses. They lived happily; and if we live as happily we shall do well.

12 · The Blackstairs Mountain

Once upon a time a poor widow and her granddaughter lived in a tiny house on the top of a hill. From the windows of this tiny house you could see down into a green valley, and across the valley to a great mountain called the Blackstairs. Witches lived on the mountain. So every night, before they went to bed, the widow and her granddaughter did four things.

This is what they did: first, they loosed the band that worked the spinning wheel and laid it on the wheel-seat; second, they emptied the washing water into a channel that ran under the house door; third, they covered the burning turf on the hearth with ashes; fourth, they took the broom and pushed the handle of it through the bolt sockets of the house door, where the bolt itself had long ago rusted away. And, having done all that, they went to bed and slept soundly, knowing that the witches could not get in. Because the doing of these things formed a spell to keep the witches out.

But one day the widow and her granddaughter went to market, to sell the linen thread they had spun. It was a wild, wild day, and a wilder night. Coming home, they took shelter from a storm of rain under some trees; and by the time the rain had eased off a bit, it was night; they missed their way in the dark, and didn't get home till very late.

When they did get home, they were so weary that their one thought was to get to bed; and they forgot all about the doing of those four things that they should have done to keep the witches out.

Well, they ate a sup and they drank a sup, and were making to go to their beds when there came four loud bangs on the house door. They were making for the door then, to see who was knocking, when a voice screamed out of the night; and it was such an unholy scream that the widow and her granddaughter stood still in the middle of the kitchen and clutched each other in fear.

'Where are you, washing water?' screamed the voice.

And the washing water answered, 'I am here in the tub.'

'Where are you, spinning wheel band?' screamed the voice.

And the wheel band answered, 'I am here, fast round the wheel, as if it was spinning.'

'Broom, where are you?' screamed the voice.

And the broom answered, 'I am here, with my handle in the dustpan.'

'Turf coal, where are *you*?' screamed the voice.

And the burning turf answered, 'I am here, blazing over the ashes.'

Then – *bang, bang, bang, bang* at the door again, and a score of hideous voices howled, 'Washing water, wheel band, broom, and turf coal, let us in!'

The door flew open: in rushed a great company of witches; and in their midst, leaping and yelling, was old Nick himself, with his red horns and his green tail.

Pandemonium! Witches all round them, whirling about the kitchen, whooping, bawling, yelling with laughter. The grandmother fell down in a faint, and there was the terrified granddaughter standing now in the midst of a throng of jeering, ill-favoured faces and skinny waving arms, with her poor old grandmother lying like a dead thing at her feet.

Old Nick, with the red horns and the green tail, had seated himself on a stool by the fire. He had his hands to his nose, and he was pulling that nose in and out as if it were a trombone, and making the most hideous music with it. The witches began to dance to the music, kicking up their heels, leaping till their heads cracked against the ceiling, upsetting the chairs, the table, the pots and pans, the china and the crocks. *Smash*, went the widow's best china tea pot; *smash, smash*, went cups and plates; *clitter, clatter, smash, smash* – everything was tumbling off the dresser. The very dresser itself

reeled and swayed and toppled sideways against the window, and the window panes fell out with a crash.

'Oh what shall I do, what *shall* I do?' thought the poor terrified granddaughter. 'Oh, if granny should die! If this goes on till cockcrow granny *will* die – she will never live to see another day! I must do something – but what *can* I do?'

Then an idea came to her. And if a good fairy didn't put that idea into the girl's head, then who did? The music that Old Nick was making with his nose became more and more hideous; the dance of the witches became more and more furious: screaming with laughter they leaped forth and back over the poor old grandmother, stretched on the floor in her faint. But they were taking no notice of the girl. So, holding her breath, and a step at a time, the girl sidled her way towards the house door. The door was still open. The girl slipped through it, and out into the night.

What did she do then? She screamed with all her might, rushed back into the kitchen, and shouted at the top of her voice, 'Granny, Granny, come out! The Blackstairs Mountain and the sky above it is all on fire!'

Instantly the music stopped, and the dancing stopped. Old Nick made one leap through the window; the witches crowded after him, some through the door, some through the window. Out in the night rose a great and terrible cry, as with shrieks and lamentations the witches rose into the air and sped away through the darkness towards their home on the Blackstairs Mountain.

The shrieks and lamentations dwindled away into the distance, but the granddaughter hadn't wasted one moment in listening to them. Directly the last witch was out of the house, she seized up the broom and clapped the handle of it through the sockets where the door-bolt ought to be. Then she dragged the tub of washing water across the kitchen, and emptied the water into the channel under the house door. Then she loosed the band of the spinning wheel and laid it on the wheel-seat; and last, she raked the ashes in the hearth over the burning turf, till not one red ember could be seen. Having done all that, she ran to her granny and brought her to her senses by dashing cold water in her face.

The grandmother sat up. 'Is all quiet at last?' she said.

'Yes, all is quiet,' said the girl.

But no: from out in the night came a distant angry roaring; and the roaring grew nearer and nearer and louder and louder, as the witches came whirling back from their home, furious at the trick the girl had played on them.

The roar ended in sudden silence. Then – *tap, tap, tap, tap:* four quiet little knocks on the door.

'Washing water, let me in!' came a wheedling, whispering voice.

But the washing water answered, 'I can't; I am spilled into the channel under the door. I am trickling away round your feet, and my path is down to the valley.'

'Spinning wheel band, *you* let me in!' came the wheedling voice.

But the wheel band answered, 'I can't; I am lying loose on the wheel-seat.'

'Broom, let me in!' whispered the wheedling voice.

'I can't,' answered the broom. 'I am put here to bolt the door.'

'Turf coal, turf coal, open to me, open!' urged the whispering wheedling voice.

And the hot turf answered, 'I can't; my head is smothered with ashes.'

Then came such a howling and cursing outside the door as made the widow and her granddaughter fall on their knees and cling together. But, howl and curse as they might, the witches could not get in. They whirled away through the night at last, back to their home on the Blackstairs Mountain.

The widow and her granddaughter had a job of it putting their house to rights. But you may be sure, after that night, never again did they go to their beds until they had loosed the spinning wheel band, emptied the washing water, piled ashes over the hot turf, and pushed the handle of the broom through the bolt sockets on the door.